Scottish Folk Tales

Scottish Folk Tales

RUTH MANNING-SANDERS

Illustrated by William Stobbs

Methuen Children's Books · London

First published in Great Britain 1976
by Methuen Children's Books Ltd
11 New Fetter Lane, London EC4P 4EE
Text copyright © 1976 Ruth Manning-Sanders
Illustrations copyright © 1976
Methuen Children's Books Ltd
Printed in Great Britain
by Fletcher & Son Ltd, Norwich, Norfolk
ISBN 0 416 82580 X

Contents

Foreword

When we were children, my sisters and I, we spent our summer holidays in a farmhouse at the edge of a sea loch in the Highlands. The farmer's family was a big one, ranging from Granny Stewart (very old, very lame, and generally laughing) down through parents, grown-up sons and daughters, to children of our own age.

Granny Stewart knew no end of stories, and she loved to tell them as much as we loved to listen. It is her version of some of these Scottish fairy tales that I am now telling. Not that she invented them: they are age-old stories, and come from various parts of Scotland.

For instance: *The seal-hunter* comes from John O' Groats, *Mester Stoorworm* and *Flitting* from the Orkney Islands. From the west coast come *Seven Inches, Green caps, Whirra whirra bump!* and *The Laird of Co* (Co because of the Coes or caves in the rock on which the laird's castle was built). From eastern Scotland come *My own self, The shadow, Short Hoggers* and *The little wee man*. From the Border country come *The Well at the World's End, In a sack* and *The Black Bull of Norroway*. As to the *Loch Ness Kelpie*, we all know about *him*! Apparently he still lives in that big loch under the mountains in Inverness.

7

Of course we weren't always listening to stories: that was a wet weather pastime. At other times we were out swimming, or riding the farm horses (when they allowed themselves to be caught) or boating on the loch and singing to the seals. The seals lived on a small rocky island, and if we sang as we rowed past this island they would plump off the rocks into the water and follow the boat. We could watch their round heads, with their bright shining eyes, lifting above the water, and disappearing, and appearing again, for as long as we chose to sing to them – a compliment our singing scarcely merited!

The evenings would usually find us gathered in the big candle-lit barn, with one of the grown-up sons (either Jock or Lachie) marching up and down playing the bagpipes, and all the rest of us energetically dancing reels.

What fun we had! But I think the highlight of all these holidays came on my tenth birthday. On the evening before this birthday (unknown to us children) a gipsy with a dancing bear arrived at the farm, asking to be ferried across the loch. With a good supper of cheese and oatcakes, and a bed of straw in a disused stable, the gipsy was easily persuaded to stay the night. Imagine my joyous surprise when, on running out next morning after breakfast, I saw the bear on a grass plat close to the quay, waiting to go through his tricks. And go through his tricks with a will he did, to the applause of a little crowd of spectators – ourselves and all the Stewart family.

And when the tricks had been duly performed, with ample rewards of 'sugar and spice and all things nice' between each one, the bear was led down to the waiting boat, clambered in, and seated himself in the stern, like the seasoned traveller he was.

I remember it so vividly: the bear with his humped brown back and heavy head, the two rowers watching his every movement rather anxiously, and ourselves standing in a group on the quay, shouting our farewells.

But not once did that bear turn to give us a parting glance. His eyes were fixed on the opposite shore, where doubtless he would go through his performance all over again: though never, surely, to a more appreciative audience. . . .

(The name of the farm, by the way, was *Shian*, which means the place where fairies live.)

Scottish Folk Tales

1 My own self

'Percy Armstrong, get to your bed.'
  'No!'
  'Percy Armstrong, do you hear what I say?'
  'Aye. I hear.'
  'Well then, are you going to your bed?'
  '*No!*'

'Percy Armstrong, if you don't go to your bed, the old fairy-wife will get you.'

'Let her try!'

'Percy Armstrong, if you don't get to your bed, I will go to mine and leave you.'

'Och – go then!'

So Percy Armstrong's mother went to bed, and left the little laddie Percy sitting on the kitchen floor in front of the fire.

And he hadn't been sitting there very long when he heard a *huffle-wuffle* in the chimney, and down on to the hearth jumped a teeny-tiny fairy girl, no bigger than a doll, with silvery hair, and grass-green eyes, and cheeks the colour of a linnet's breast.

'Oh!' said Percy. And, 'Oh' says he again. 'And what might they be calling you?'

'Just my own self,' said the teeny-tiny fairy girl, in a sweet little chirruping teeny-tiny voice. 'And what will they be calling *you*?'

'Just my own self, too,' says Percy.

And they began to play together.

The teeny-tiny fairy girl knew some fine games. She took up the ashes from the hearth in her teeny-tiny hands, and made those ashes into teeny-tiny animals and birds that ran about, and flew about, and talked and sang. She made teeny-tiny trees, and teeny-tiny houses, and teeny-tiny people, not an inch high, who looked out of the doors of their houses, and walked here and there, and chatted one to the other in oh such teeny-tiny voices! Percy laughed and clapped his hands; he couldn't have enough of such games. And just think – if he had gone to bed, as his mother had bidden him, he would have missed all this!

Well now, by and by the fire burned low, and the light from it was getting dim. Percy couldn't see so well what the teeny-tiny fairy girl was doing. So he took up a stick and stirred the coals; and there – if a hot cinder didn't go and fall on to the teeny-tiny girl's teeny-tiny foot!

Oh, oh, oh – what a screech she gave! It was like all the winds in the world whistling through a teeny-tiny keyhole.

That screech gave Percy a fright! He had just taken a leap to hide himself under the table, when a huge great voice sounded in the chimney: 'What's to do there? Who is it screeching?'

'Just my own self,' blubbered the teeny-tiny girl. 'My . . . my f-foot's burned sore with a h-hot c-cinder!'

'And who did that?' roared the huge great voice, very angry, in the chimney.

'Just my own self, too,' whimpered the fairy girl.

'Then if you did it your own self,' shouted the voice in the chimney, 'what's the use of making such a fash about it?'

And Percy, peeping from under the table, saw a great hand, on the end of a long skinny arm, poking out from down the chimney.

The great hand seized the teeny-tiny fairy girl by one ear, gave the teeny-tiny girl a shake, and pulled her up the chimney out of sight.

Percy could still hear her squealing. Quicker than quick he ran to his bed, and dived down under the blankets.

Next night, when his mother told him it was time for bed, Percy was willing enough to go. For who knows what might not have happened when she of the great hand and arm got to know the truth of the matter?

2 The Laird of Co

One sunny morning the good Laird of Co was taking a stroll about his castle grounds; and there came to him a wee laddie, dangling a tin pannikin on his arm.

'If ye please, Laird of Co,' says the wee laddie, 'my mither lies sick in the bed, and if ye could spare her a drop of ale, I'm thinking 'twould do her good.'

'Why, of course she shall have some ale,' said the Laird of Co. 'Go to the kitchen, laddie, and ask the butler to fill your pannikin full with the best ale in my cellar. Say I sent you.'

So off runs the wee laddie to the castle kitchen, finds the butler, and gives him the laird's message. The butler takes the laddie down to the wine cellar. Well, well, the *best* ale did the laird say? That would be in the barrel that was specially kept for the laird's own drinking. 'A pity,' thought the butler, 'to waste that on a poor woman who wouldn't know the best from the worst!' However, the master's orders must be obeyed. And, after all, that little pannikin wouldn't hold more than a pint, if that.

So the butler took the pannikin from the wee laddie, held it under the tap of the barrel with one hand, and turned the tap with the other hand. Out came the ale in a golden stream, *ripple, ripple, ripple, ripple*; and out it came, and out it came – but what was this? The barrel was swiftly emptying itself, but the little pannikin was not yet half full! Plague on it, this was sheer witchery; the laddie must be a bogle, and his mother no better! The butler didn't like it – no, he did *not*! 'Here, take your ale and be off with ye,' says he to the wee laddie.

'But my pannikin is not yet full,' says the wee laddie.

'It's full enough,' says the butler. 'It's emptied the cask!'

'The laird said I was to have my pannikin full,' says the wee laddie.

'And how am I to fill it if it won't fill?' cries the butler. 'It's witchery! Away with you and take your witchery some place else!'

'The laird said I was to have my pannikin full,' said the wee laddie again.

'Be off, ere I give you a clout!' says the butler.

'The laird said I was to have my pannikin full,' said the wee laddie.

No, he wouldn't budge. So the butler hurried off to tell

the Laird of Co that he had a bogle in the cellar.

But the laird only laughed. 'I did tell the laddie he should have his pannikin full,' said he. 'And have it full he shall, if it takes all the ale in my cellar. So go back and broach another cask.'

The butler's teeth were chattering, and his hair was standing on end. 'I'm afeared the wee bogle bodes us no good,' said he.

'Pooh!' said the Laird of Co. 'Do as you're bid.'

So the butler went down to the cellar again, and broached another cask. 'Give us that dommed pannikin of yours,' says he to the wee laddie.

The laddie handed him the pannikin. What happened this time? Scarcely had the butler held it under the tap of the newly broached barrel, when the pannikin was full to the brim. The laddie took the full pannikin and off with him: up out of the cellar, and through the castle grounds, skipping along past the Laird of Co, with a 'Good day to ye!' and so out of sight behind a copse of elders. And though the good laird asked this one and the other one about the laddie and his mother, thinking they might be in need of help, not one of those he asked had ever heard tell of them, much less set eyes on them.

Well, the years passed; and there came a day when war broke out between the laird's country and a foreign country. Then the Laird of Co put on his armour, and crossed the sea to fight for his country, like the brave man he was. But though he fought valiantly, he was taken prisoner, and shut up in jail, and condemned to death.

So there he was, on the night before his execution, lying on the dank floor of his prison cell, and thinking of his home: of his castle and his pleasant grounds, and the rivers and lochs and mountains of his beloved country which he would never see again. And there came into his mind a memory of one sunny morning, of himself strolling on the green lawn in front of his castle, of the daisies winking in the sun and wind, and of a wee laddie stepping towards him over the daisied grass, dangling a pannikin on his arm.

Such a clear picture the laird had of that wee laddie – he could almost see him now. . . . *Almost* see him? *But he was seeing him!* The door of the prison cell had opened without a sound, and there was the wee laddie stepping noiselessly over the straw-littered floor with his finger to his lip.

And the wee laddie whispered:

> *'Laird o' Co,*
> *Rise and go!*
> *If ye'd be free,*
> *Follow me!'*

Like a man in a dream the Laird of Co got to his feet and followed the wee laddie out through the open door, down one long passage, and another long passage, through locked doors that opened at the wee laddie's touch, past prison guards who lay snoring at their posts, out into the prison yard, and through the great barred gates that swung open noiselessly to let them pass.

'Now, Laird o' Co,' said the wee laddie, 'get ye on my back.'

'*I* get on *your* back, my little one?'

'Yes, on my back.'

'I am surely dreaming,' said the Laird of Co, as he set his long legs across the wee laddie's back,

> *'For never waking one so tall*
> *Could ride upon a back so small!'*

But ride upon that back he did, and away went the wee laddie over the land, over the water, over the moors, over the mountains, and never stopped till he set the laird down in front of his own castle, on his own green lawn, where the daisies were winking in the sun and wind.

The wee laddie was laughing. He looked up at the Laird of Co, and said:

'Ae good turn deserves anither,
I to ye, ye to my mither.'

And with that he gave a hop and a skip, and vanished.
Nor did the Laird of Co ever see that wee laddie again.

3 The shadow

Jamie Carmichael was a bright lad; and when his grandad died and left him a purseful of money nothing would content Jamie but that he must away to Maister Orrack's Academy, to learn all that Maister Orrack could teach him in the way of magic.

'Oh no, no, no!' said Jamie's father.

And 'Oh no, no, no!' said Jamie's mother. 'Have you not heard that Maister Orrack is no other than the Devil himself?'

'And who's afraid o' the Devil?' says Jamie. 'Not this laddie!'

So off he goes, with a stout holly stick in his hand, and a change of linen in a bundle on his back, and the purse in his pocket. Over the mountain and over the moor he goes, sleeps that night in the heather, and comes next morning to Maister Orrack's place – a grand enough building set in a valley between two heathy hills. And it's *rat, tat, tat* on the front door with Jamie's holly stick, and the door opening, and Maister Orrack himself looking out.

'What's your will, my laddie?' says Maister Orrack.

'To learn all you can teach me,' says Jamie.

'It'll cost you a bittock,' says Maister Orrack.

'And it's I have the money to pay,' says Jamie.

'Well, come your ways in,' says Maister Orrack, 'and sit you doon till you hear the terms of my schooling. They're not to every lad's liking.'

'If they're to mine, that'll be all that's needful,' says Jamie, stepping into a great hall, where he took one seat, and Maister Orrack another.

So now there's Jamie, sitting to listen, and there's Maister Orrack unrolling a parchment, and reading out the rules that all his pupils had to obey.

The rules were under thirteen headings. There were rules about times of rising, and times of going to bed, and rules about attendance at classes, and rules about behaviour, and what was permitted in the leisure hours. It all sounded fair and square enough to Jamie: until Maister Orrack read out the thirteenth and last rule, which was none other than this – that when at the end of their schooling the pupils took their leave, the last one out of the house was to belong, body and soul, and for all eternity, to Maister Orrack.

'Hech sirs!' says Jamie. 'That takes some swallowing!'

'Take it or leave it,' says Maister Orrack. 'If you're liking my terms you'll sign here, at the bottom of the parchment. If you're not liking my terms, it's good day to you.'

'Gie me a wee minute to consider on it,' says Jamie.

'I'll gie you five, and no more,' says Maister Orrack.

Jamie sat thinking. His eyes wandered round the great hall. He looked at the great open door, he looked up at the great windows. It was noonday, and the sun shone in at the door and in through the windows, casting the shadows of the chairs and the table, and of himself and of Maister Orrack along the floor behind them.

'Is it through this hall and out at that door the scholars will be leaving when they do leave?' says Jamie.

'Aye,' says Maister Orrack.

'And at what time do they leave?' says Jamie.

'Just about this time,' says Maister Orrack.

'Hand over the scroll then, and I'll sign,' says Jamie; 'trusting that since I've a good pair of legs I shan't be the last man out.'

'That's what they all say,' answered Maister Orrack. And he took a quill pen from behind his ear, unscrewed the stopper of a small flask that hung by a gold chain from his girdle, dipped the pen in the flask, handed the pen to Jamie, and laid the scroll flat on the table.

'Sign here,' says he.

So Jamie signed his name, and looked at what he had written. 'It's unco' red; I jalouse it's blood,' says he.

'You're about right, smart laddie,' says Maister Orrack. 'Will you be paying the fees now, or on the day you leave?'

'I'll be paying now, and have it off my mind,' says Jamie, 'for it seems that on the day I leave I may be in a hurry.' And he handed his purse to Maister Orrack. 'Take what it costs,' says he.

'It costs all that and a bittock more, if you had more,' says Maister Orrack, putting the purse in his pocket. 'But come your ways now, and get acquainted with your fellow

23

scholars.'

So saying, he led Jamie into another great room, where some thirty young fellows sat at desks with open books before them. They all sprang to their feet when Maister Orrack came in.

'A new scholar,' says Maister Orrack. 'By name Jamie Carmichael. Bid him welcome, my lads.'

'Welcome to you, welcome, Jamie Carmichael!' cried the lads. Their voices echoed round the great room and then fell silent.

'You can take your seats again,' says Maister Orrack.

And like so many well-drilled soldiers, they all sat.

Maister Orrack showed Jamie to an empty desk, bade him be seated, and himself took his stand on a platform at the top of the room.

'This morning, laddies,' says he, 'I shall test you in the art of transformation. You, Jock Craddock, become a goshawk, you, Tammy Croker, a tiger, you, Bill Macduff, a dog; the lave of you sheep, goats, cats, bats, rats – any shape you fancy.'

Well, immediately the room echoed with strange cries, and every scholar vanished; in their places there were lions roaring, and cats mewing, and pigs grunting, and dogs barking, and bats and all manner of birds flying overhead. Jamie was so excited that he shouted, 'Hurrah!' And then Maister Orrack clapped his hands, and the birds and beasts and bats all vanished: there were the scholars sitting demurely at their desks again; all except one queer creature that was tumbling about on the floor, with a lad's head and hands on it, and the legs and body of a weasel.

'Sandy MacNab, ye'll stay in and study your book with more profit,' said Maister Orrack, giving the queer creature a touch with his pointed boot, and turning it into a very crestfallen lad. 'The rest of you, dismiss till dinner time. And take the new scholar with you. You'll have plenty to say to him, no doubt. And you can give me a good name or a bad name according to your fancies,' says he with a chuckle.

Then out scampered all the lads but one, and out scampered Jamie after them, in a fine state of excitement at what he had seen, and more excited still at what he now saw. For the lads were showing off to Jamie: some riding through the air on stalks of ragwort that obligingly turned themselves into little winged horses; some doing the vanishing trick – one moment there, one moment gone, next moment there again; some gathering up a handful of pebbles and turning those pebbles into a swarm of bees; and yet others scaling an invisible ladder and hailing Jamie from above his head.

'Oh mannies!' says Jamie, 'oh mannies! It's I that will be the right good scholar, and beat you all at these games before the year's out!'

Well, Jamie did become a right good scholar, and learned all the magic that Maister Orrack was willing to teach him. 'You'll make a braw wizard of yourself, my laddie,' said Maister Orrack; 'second only to myself, when you win away from here. *If* you win away,' says he with a crooked smile. 'And if you'll not win away, I've never a doubt but that my acquaintances down below will be glad to receive you.'

'I'm not intending to pay them a visit,' says Jamie.

'Are you not?' says Maister Orrack. 'It's either you or some other lad, I'm thinking.'

That was the trouble: and as the days passed, and the weeks passed, and the months passed, the high spirits of Maister Orrack's pupils dwindled with every hour. For they had all signed that contract with its ominous thirteenth clause, and who could tell which of them was doomed at the year's end to belong, body and soul, and to all eternity, to their terrible master? Instead of laughter and merry faces and friendliness, there were now scowling looks and tremblings and a creeping away into corners, and frequent quarrellings. 'For oh, if it should be myself last out!' each one was thinking. 'And oh, if it could only be the other fellow!'

25

But none of this seemed to worry Jamie. And one day, in the leisure hour, he called his comrades together, and made them a speech. 'Friends,' says he, 'it's I that am not liking your troubled faces. And it's I that am making you a promise. When the time comes, I pledge you my word that you shall all go out before me.'

'You cannot mean it!' they cried.

'Indeed and I do mean it,' says Jamie. 'I am no more fearing Maister Orrack than I am fearing one of my mither's geese.'

'But it's hell and damnation!' cried one.

'And to all eternity!' cried another.

'Away wi' your hell and damnation,' says Jamie. 'And away wi' your all eternity! There's that cunning in me can defy all.'

It took the lads a while to believe that Jamie was in earnest, but they did come to believe it, and then all was well. Now they regarded Jamie as a hero, and the frowns and frightened looks turned into smiles and merriment again. And so the days slid by, and the day came when Maister Orrack summoned his scholars into the great hall to take their leave of him.

Maister Orrack had drawn a chalk line across the hall, and had all his scholars standing behind the line, each with a right foot touching the chalk. It was just such a bright summer morning as the morning on which Jamie had first come to the Academy; and the sun was shining through the great open door, casting the shadows of Maister Orrack and of all the pupils along the floor behind them.

'Now, my laddies,' says Maister Orrack, 'I've taught you all I can, and made canny wizards of the lot of you. I have your signed parchments, and you know what for you have signed. Here's a wee gong I'm holding in my hand. When I strike the gong, you'll make a run to get through the door. If I were a grasping and deceitful sort of fellow, I could hold the lot of you to do my will for ever and aye.

But I'm only claiming the last laddie out, according to the contract.'

And with that Maister Orrack strikes the gong, and there's a rush to the door, each lad for his life, and a pushing and an elbowing and a scrambling, and a getting through that door all in a heap, and a rushing off across the heather pell-mell, and never pausing until they had reached the end of the valley, and Maister Orrack's Academy was just a little wee speck in the distance behind them.

But back in the great hall of Maister Orrack's Academy, there was Jamie, sauntering in the sunlight across the floor towards the door, as if he had all the day before him. And there was Maister Orrack, with an evil grin on his face, reaching out a hand to take a hold of Jamie's shoulder.

'Hands off!' says Jamie.

'Hands off, is it?' says Maister Orrack. 'That's no way to talk! I have your contract signed with the best blood; and being the last to leave, you belong to me. And to all eternity!' he added with a high cackle of laughter.

'Ah, but I am not the last to leave,' says Jamie.

'*Not the last!*' says Maister Orrack. 'And who is it that's leaving after you, if I may ask?'

'Take a look on the ground,' says Jamie strolling to the door. 'It's there you'll see the one that's coming behind me.'

'There's none coming behind you,' says Maister Orrack.

'What? Not my shadow?' says Jamie. 'He's the fellow that's the last to leave – and you're welcome to him. So I'll bid you a good morning, Maister Orrack, thanking you kindly for all you've taught me.'

And off strolls Jamie out through the door and down the valley in the bright sunshine. A little breeze set the shadows of the gorse bushes and heather clumps and fronds of bracken wavering across Jamie's path, both before and behind him, and on either side. But where was Jamie's shadow? Neither before nor behind him, nor on either side. It lay where Jamie had left it, on the floor of Maister Orrack's great hall.

Maister Orrack stooped and took the shadow into himself. 'Ah, Jamie Carmichael,' he sighed. 'I wadna have lost you for all the souls in hell! It's a braw canny wizard you'll be making when you come to be a man!'

And a braw canny wizard Jamie became: famed throughout the country for his curious knowledge, and for his healing of folks' ailments, and for advising them always for their good and never for their ill. *Maister Carmichael the Good, the Man without a Shadow*, was the name he went by.

4 The wee bit mousikie

There was a wee bit mousikie,
That lived in Gilberaty, O.
It couldna get a bite o' cheese,
For cheetie-poussie-cattie, O.

The mouse said to the cheesikie,
'Oh fain wad I be at ye, O,
If it were na for the cruel paws
O' cheetie-poussie-cattie, O.'

5 Green caps

Jock Gowrie and his wife, Meg, lived in a little two-roomed house on a grassy place by the sea. They had a little garden and little croft, a cock, a few hens, a couple of geese and a pig. They were working hard all the hours of daylight, what with one thing and another: growing peas and beans and lettuces in the garden, and turnips and cabbages and potatoes in the croft. And on sunny evenings, Jock went fishing off the rocks: no, they hadn't a boat, they couldn't afford one.

All the same, Jock thought they did well enough. But Meg would sometimes sigh and say, 'One day and another day, and no better off tomorrow than today! And oh, my man, I am often wearying after pretty things!'

'Well,' says Jock, 'there's plenty of them around – flowers and birds and that ilk.'

'*Flowers and birds!*' says she. 'I mean in the house – yours and mine.'

So then Jock goes out and picks a bunch of bluebells, brings them into the kitchen, and says, 'Here's something pretty for you!'

And she laughs and says, 'You're a darling man, Jock Gowrie, and I'm a silly woman.'

Well now, early one morning, Jock went out gathering sticks to kindle the kitchen fire. And as he was going through a coppice of hazel trees he heard the sound of shrill laughter, *ha! ha! ha!* and *ho! ho! ho!*, coming from a little dell on the seaward side of him. Who could be there in this lonesome place, where scarce a body ever came? Jock was curious. He laid his bundle of sticks under a hazel bush, and went pushing his way through a high growth of bracken down a steep path that led to the dell. And first he heard the laughter, and then he heard a frightened squealing, and the patter of lightly running feet. And when he got into the dell, not a soul did he see.

But something he did see: and that was a small green hillock; and lying on the grass at the foot of the hillock were four silver goblets, four silver spoons, and a big silver dish.

'Oh! Oh!' Jock was down on his knees, picking up one silver thing after another, turning them over in his hands, marvelling at their beauty. 'Oh! Oh! If these were but mine,' thinks he, 'I would carry them home to Meg and watch the pleasure waken in her eyes!'

31

But Jock was an honest fellow, and finding was not necessarily keeping. So, with many a sigh, he left the lovely things where he found them, pushed his way up from the dell through the bracken, and went home with his bundle of sticks.

When he told Meg what he had seen, she said, 'How d'you know the pretty things weren't meant for us? Or how d'you know that those who owned them haven't gone their ways without them? How d'you know that they won't lie there till they rust? Get you back and see are they still there.'

'Nay,' says Jock, 'there's work to be done. I can't go sluggarding off again at this time of day! . . . Oh, all right,' (for Meg was beginning to whimper) 'don't fret, I'll go come gloaming.'

So, when the day's work was done, and the sun had set, and twilight coming on, and the moon rising, Jock went down to the dell again. This time he went very cautiously, very quietly, stooping and creeping under the bracken, hoping to see and not be seen, should the owners of the pretty silver things be anywhere about. There he was now, crouched and hidden, but in sight of the green knoll; and yes, the pretty things, all bright and glittering in the moonlight, were still lying where he had seen them in the morning.

And hark – what was that? The shrill laughter again! And see, what was happening? A door in the green knoll opened, and out stepped a crowd of tiny men, dressed in green, and each holding a green cap in his hand.

The tiny green men went over to the pretty silver things, and looked at them a while in silence. Then one of them piped up, 'I see, I see – what do I see? I see the prints of fingers on our bonny treasures! I hear, I hear – what do I hear? I hear a sigh rising from them, and an unspoken wish – a wish that the one who fingered them might e'en call them his own, and carry them away.'

'Then why didn't he carry them away?' piped another tiny man.

'Because he thought it would be thieving,' said the first tiny man.

'Then someone's a good fellow!' said the second tiny man.

'Well then, let someone have our treasures!' shrilled a third tiny man. 'They're no use to us now,

> *For treasure touched by human hand*
> *Cannot stay in the Green Land.'*

'And we can get plenty more where these came from!' laughed another tiny man. And he put on his green cap. *'Ho and away for London town!'* he cried, and rose up into the air like a bird.

Then all the other tiny men put on their green caps.

'Ho and away for London town!' they cried. And up into the air with them, light as thistledown, floating away and away, over the bracken, over the green knoll, over the hazel coppice, and out of sight.

Now everything was silent: not a leaf stirred, not an owl hooted, not a fox barked. But there were the pretty silver things lying at the foot of the hillock, all bright and glittering in the moonlight, and there was Jock crouched under the bracken, and wondering was he awake or dreaming. But dreaming or waking, he was very sure that he had heard aright, and that he was the 'someone' whom the little fellows in the green caps had said might have their treasure.

So, without more ado, he came out from under the bracken, gathered up the silver goblets, and the silver spoons, and the silver dish, and off home with him, fast as he could pelt, to carry the treasures to Meg . . . and to see what he delighted to see, 'the pleasure waken in her eyes.'

But when she had hugged Jock, and laughed and clapped her hands, and shed some happy tears, and arranged the silver dish and the silver goblets and the silver spoons on a shelf opposite the window in the kitchen, where tomorrow's morning sun could waken twinkling lights in them – when all that was done to her satisfaction, Meg became thoughtful.

If the kitchen had looked mean and poorly furnished in her eyes before the coming of those silver things, it looked a hundred times meaner and poorer now by contrast. The curtains at the window – oh, how dull and drab! And those two wooden chairs – the only chairs that Meg and Jock possessed – how stolidly ugly! And the teapot had a broken spout, and as to the cups and plates – well, no one would give twopence for them at a rag fair! So what between delight in her new treasure, and sorrow over her old possessions, Meg couldn't sleep that night: she was tossing and turning and sighing, and feeling unreasonably annoyed with Jock, who slept so peacefully at her side.

And then she had an idea!

All next day she was brooding over that idea; and at sunset, when Jock had taken his fishing tackle and gone down to the rocks to catch something for next day's dinner, what did she do? She packed most of her crockery into a sack, slung the sack over her shoulder, took a chair in either hand, and off with her down to the dell.

And there, in front of the green knoll she set down the chairs and the sackful of crockery, whispered, 'A present for those who made a present to us,' and off home with her again, fast as her legs would carry her.

By and by in comes Jock with a catch of sea trout. But when he goes to sit down – well, there isn't a chair to sit on. And when Meg brings him a drink of tea – well there, she brings it in a tin mug. And when he glances at the window – well there, the curtains are gone. 'What's come to everything?' says he, wrinkling up his forehead.

Then Meg laughs and tells him what she's done. 'And first thing in the morning, my man,' says she, 'we'll away down to the dell, to see is there anything waiting for us there. There *will* be something waiting, or I'm much mistook.'

No, Meg wasn't mistaken. They were up before the sun, and hastening off to the dell. And when they got down there

– what did they see? They didn't see what Meg had left there, certainly. They saw something much better: two handsome oak chairs with padded cushions, a set of the prettiest crockery anyone could imagine, elegantly patterned with pink roses, and two velvet window curtains striped with gold and green.

'Can these things be for us?' says Jock. 'Is it a gift, think you?'

And from out of the green knoll came a titter of laughter, and a little squeaky voice, 'Yes, yes, a gift for a good fellow and his wee wifey.'

So Jock picked up the chairs, and Meg packed the crockery into the sack; and so, Jock carrying the chairs and she the crockery and the curtains, off home with them again.

Now when the curtains were hung, and the crockery neatly arranged, and the handsome chairs set one on each side of the hearth, the kitchen looked more as a kitchen should look. In fact, as Meg said, it was a dream of a kitchen. But what about the bedroom, with its crazy old bed, and darned sheets, and patched blankets? No, that did nobody any credit!

'Do you ken what I'm thinking?' said Meg, as she put on her nightgown that evening. 'I'm thinking we'll be carrying the bed down to the dell tomorrow morning.'

'Aye, might so well,' says Jock, laughing.

'And the cracked old looking-glass,' said Meg, 'and the tin washbowl, and everything else in the room. Oh Jock, I'm going to be a proud housewife from this time forth!'

So in the morning off with them to the dell again, going forth and back several times, lugging the bed and the sheets and blankets and the rest of the bedroom furniture. And in the evening again visiting the dell, and finding there a handsome oak bedstead and four beautiful soft white woolly blankets, an embroidered bedcover, six snow-white sheets, pretty window curtains, a gay carpet, a carved chest, chairs to match, a marble washstand, an ivory washbasin, a looking-glass in a silver frame, a silver comb and a silver-backed hairbrush: bedroom furniture, as Meg said, fit for the king of England himself.

It did Jock good to see Meg's happy face, as she bustled about the cottage, arranging and rearranging all their new treasures. And when she said they ought to show their gratitude to the little men, Jock heartily agreed with her. So Meg did a baking of cakes and scones, and tarts and sweetmeats, enough to fill two large baskets; and in the evening Jock carried the baskets down to the dell, and left them outside the green knoll, with a big THANK YOU scrawled on a sheet of paper by their side. . . .

'I wonder,' said Meg next morning, 'did the wee men take pleasure in my baking? Anyways, Jock, go and fetch back the baskets. . . . And maybe,' says she laughing, 'there's been something put in them for us.'

'Nay,' says Jock, 'they've given us plenty.'

'So they have,' says she. 'I was but joking. But go you now and bring back the empty baskets.'

'And how many more times will I be pushing my way down through the thorns and bracken to that place?' says Jock laughing.

And off with him down to the dell.

Yes, the baskets were where he and Meg had left them, and they were empty; and lying beside one of them was a tiny green cap.

'Somebody's dropped that,' thinks Jock. And then he thought again. 'Maybe somebody left it there for a purpose?'

But for what purpose? Jock picked up the tiny cap and turned it in his hands. And even as he did so, that cap grew bigger and still bigger. . . . 'Why, I believe 'twould 'most fit me,' thinks Jock, and he puts it on his head. 'Yes, it fits.'

And what was it the little men said when they put on their caps? ' "Ho and away for London town," that's what they said!' exclaimed Jock.

And no sooner had he said those words than there he was up in the air, and through the clouds, and above the clouds, and skimming away over moor and mountain, over rivers and lakes, over forests and farms and towns and hamlets, fast, fast, faster – till he was dizzy with his going and had to shut his eyes.

Bump! Down to earth with him again. And where was he now? Where but in London town! Where but in the cellar of the king's palace! And he hadn't been there long before the cellar door was flung open, and in stamped two fierce-looking men with drawn swords in their hands.

'Ha! Thief! So we've caught you at last!' shouted one of the fierce-looking men. And the two of them seized Jock by the arms and marched him off to prison. And from prison Jock was brought before a judge and jury, and accused of stealing the silver goblets and the silver spoons and the silver dish and the chairs and curtains and furniture – all the beautiful things that the little green men had given to him and Meg.

And the worst of it was that since the judge spoke only English and Jock knew only the Gaelic, he couldn't understand a word of what the judge was saying, nor could the judge understand a word of what Jock was saying, when he tried to explain how he had come to be in the cellar.

And the end of it was that the jury decided that Jock must be a wizard – for how else could he have made away with all those things? And as a wizard the judge condemned poor Jock to be hanged forthwith.

So there are the gallows set up, and there is our Jock being pushed up the steps on to the wooden platform where the gallows stand, with the hangman waiting to put the noose round Jock's neck, a great crowd gathered below to watch the hanging, and poor Jock thinking sadly of his home and of his Meg, and of the little green men whose kindness had only brought him to this melancholy end.

But stop a minute, stop a minute! *Had* their kindness

brought him to this melancholy end? Not so! Jock had taken off his green cap out of politeness when he was brought before the judge, but that green cap is still in his pocket: and in an instant, even as the hangman is about to put the noose round Jock's neck, Jock has the cap out of his pocket and on to his head.

'*Ho, and away for home!*' he shouts.

What happens? The wooden platform gives a jerk and a heave, the hangman tumbles off the platform on to the ground, platform and gallows rise into the air, and Jock, clinging tightly to the post of the gallows, rises with it: up, up, up, through the clouds and above the clouds, fast, fast, faster, over towns and hamlets, over farms and forests, over lakes and rivers, over moor and mountain, along by the shores of the blue sea, and coming down at last, gently, gently, like a bird alighting, on the grassy flat outside Jock's home.

Now there is Meg running out of the cottage, and there is Jock loosing his hold of the gallows post and hurrying to Meg, to give her one kiss after another, and to tell her of his strange adventures.

And by and by, when they had both calmed down a bit, they went together to the dell and laid the green cap on the turf outside the green knoll. 'For it's a dangerous present to give the likes of us,' said Jock. 'Thanking you kindly all the same.'

Did they hear a tinkle of shrill laughter from inside the green knoll? Or did they not? They couldn't be sure. At any rate they left the cap lying, and when they next visited the dell, that cap was gone. Nor did they get any more presents from the little green men.

But Jock built a sturdy boat for himself out of the wood of the platform and gallows. So he was able to put to sea on fine evenings, and catch many more fish than he had done off the rocks.

6 The Well at the World's End

Once upon a time, on a hot, hot summer's day, a poor widow woman wanted to bake some bannocks, but her water tub was empty. So she says to her daughter, 'Lassie,' says she, 'get you gone to the Well at the World's End and fetch me a pail of water.'

Away went the lassie with the pail; but when she came to

the Well at the World's End, the well was dry.

Now what was the lassie to do? She had come a long way and she was tired. She sat down by the side of the well and began to cry.

And there came a Paddock, a big frog, hop, hop, hopping up out of the well. 'Lassie,' says the Paddock, 'why do you cry?'

'Oh! Oh!' says she. 'My mother sent me to this well to fetch a pail of water that she might bake some bannocks, but never a drop of water do I find.'

'Lassie,' says the Paddock, 'if you'll promise to be my wife, I'll fill your pail with water for you.'

So the lassie promised. Why not? It seemed just a joke to her. And the Paddock took the pail, went deep down into the well with it, and soon came up again with the pail full of water to the brim.

'Here you are, my wee wifey,' says he.

'Much obliged to you, my big man!' says she laughing. And she takes the pail and off home with her.

So her mother baked the bannocks, and the lassie thought no more about the Paddock until evening. But just as she and her mother were about to go to their beds, there comes a little *bumpetty bump, bumpetty bump* at the house door. And there's a voice singing out in the dark:

> '*Oh, open the door, my hinny, my heart,*
> *Oh, open the door, my own true love.*
> *Remember the promise that you and I made,*
> *Down in the meadow where we two met.*'

The lassie knew the voice right well. So when her mother said, 'Now who can that be?' the lassie answered, 'Why, it's naught but a silly Paddock.'

'Then open the door to the poor wee thing, for it's dreary and dark outside,' said her mother.

So the lassie opened the door, and the Paddock came *loup – loup – louping* in, and sat down at the side of the fire.

Then he began to sing again:

> '*Oh, give me my supper, my hinny, my heart,*
> *Oh, give me my supper, my own true love.*
> *Remember the promise that you and I made,*
> *Down in the meadow where we two met.*'

'Why would I be giving a silly, slimy Paddock any supper?' says the lassie.

'Why would you not?' says her mother. 'Give the poor Paddock a wee bit supper.'

So the lassie put a bannock and a cup of milk on the table. And the Paddock crawled up the table leg, and on to the table, and golloped down both bannock and milk.

Then he began to sing again:

> '*Oh, carry me to your bed, my hinny, my heart,*
> *Oh, carry me to your bed, my own true love.*
> *Remember the promise that you and I made,*
> *Down in the meadow where we two met.*'

Oh no! The lassie wasn't going to get into bed with a Paddock! She said she would sleep on the floor, rather. But the Paddock sang 'Oh, carry me to your bed' again and again. And the lassie's mother said, 'Do as he says, or we'll get no peace this night. What harm can a Paddock do you?'

So the lassie carried the Paddock to bed, and got into bed herself, keeping as far away from the Paddock as ever she could.

She thought she'd never sleep; but sleep she did, and so did the Paddock. And when the sun rose, she woke, and the Paddock woke. And the Paddock began to sing:

> '*Now fetch me an axe, my hinny, my heart,*
> *Now fetch me an axe, my own true love.*
> *Remember the promise that you and I made,*
> *Down in the meadow where we two met.*'

'Seems I must do as you say,' grumbled the lassie. And

she jumped out of bed, and went down to the woodshed, and fetched the axe.

'What next, my lord?' says she, mocking him.

The the Paddock began to sing again:

> *'Now chop off my head, my hinny, my heart,*
> *Now chop off my head, my own true love.*
> *Remember the promise that you and I made,*
> *Down in the meadow where we two met.'*

'Nay, nay!' says the lassie. 'You're a sore trouble to me, but I can't be doing such a cruel thing as that!'

But the Paddock put his little webbed hands together, and sang his song again and again. And when the lassie said no, and no, and *no* – well then, if the tears didn't come streaming out of that Paddock's eyes. So at last the lassie gets desperate, and gives the axe a swing.

One chop – off flies his head.

And then what happens?

Just this: it's no Paddock any more, but a handsome young prince that's standing before the lassie. And the handsome young prince is singing:

> *'Oh, kiss me and wed me, my hinny, my heart,*
> *Oh, kiss me and wed me, my own true love.*
> *Remember the promise that you and I made,*
> *Down in the meadow where we two met.'*

And the lassie did remember her promise, and glad indeed was she that she had made it. The handsome young prince told her that he had been put under a spell by a wicked witch, and couldn't be freed from it until a maiden would do his bidding for a whole night, and chop off his head at the end of it.

'So now will you wed me, my hinny, my heart?' says he.

'That I will,' says the lassie. 'If my mother agrees.'

Well, of course her mother agreed. So the prince and the lassie were married, and lived happily ever after.

7 The seal-wife

Once upon a time, and a long time ago, there was a young farmer whose farmlands bordered on the sea. He was a handsome young fellow, and well to do. Folk said, 'What are you up to, living alone as you do? You should take a wife.'

But he answered, 'No! I'm better without. Who was it got

44

Adam turned out of Paradise, I should like to know?'

Well, one summer evening the farmer went down to the seashore to take a look at the weather. The sun had not yet set, the tide was at the ebb, and in his strolling he came to a place where a big rock jutted out in the sea. On the landward side the rock was high and dry, but on the seaward side the small waves were breaking against its base. And what should the farmer hear, coming from the seaward side of the rock, but laughter and merry voices and the snatch of singing.

Now that was mighty strange, because it was a lonesome place, where you could stroll from year's end to year's end, and see nothing but birds fluttering, and rabbits playing, and the movements of your own shadow on the sand. So, very cautiously, the farmer scrambled up the landward side of the rock and peered over the top of it.

And there below him, on a flat rocky shelf, just above the water, he saw a company of young folk without a stitch of clothing on any of them. Some were stretched out sunning themselves, others with linked hands were dancing and singing. And to say those folk were beautiful would be saying nothing. Not in all the world could you have seen more lovely faces, or more shapely limbs, or more smooth white skins.

Selkies – seal-folk! Yes, that's what they were: for look, in a tidy pile, just above the water, lay the seal-skins which they had stripped off when coming out of the water – just as you might strip off your clothes when going *into* the water for a swim.

'I could do with one of those skins!' thought the farmer. 'I shall need a new warm coat before winter.' And he made a dash down on to the flat of the rock where the skins lay.

Heaven help us, what a commotion! No more merry dancing, no more happy singing. In frenzied haste each seal man and woman snatched up his or her skin, plunged back into the sea, and swam away and away, pulling on their seal-skins as they went.

45

Ah ha! But the farmer had managed to grab one skin, and tucking it under his arm he made for home. But he hadn't gone far when he heard a sad, sad sound of weeping and lamenting behind him, and, turning, saw a naked lassie following him up the sand. She was holding out her little white hands, and big tears were running down over her cheeks.

'Oh, bonnie man,' she sobbed, 'have mercy on me! Give me back my skin, and I will bless you through all the years of my life!'

Now the lassie was very beautiful, and though something stirred in the farmer's heart at the sight of her, it was not pity, it was love. Yes, he who had scorned womenfolk all his life was in love at last. Forgetting all about who it was that got Adam turned out of Paradise, he took the lassie by the hand and said, 'I will never give you back your skin; you shall never go back into the sea; you shall live with me and be my wife.'

And, willy nilly, so it was: he lifted her in his arms, carried her up to the farm, wrapped her in a plaid, gave her a supper of milk and bannocks, and showed her to a bed, where she lay weeping all through the night.

Next day he rode off to town, and bought her some pretty clothes. And as soon as might be, he married her. But he hid the seal-skin away in a safe place, where he reckoned she would never find it.

So what could the poor lassie do but make the best of it? He was a kind husband, and she soon learned to do all the things about the farm that a farmer's wife must do. If she was not exactly happy with him, still she was not exactly unhappy.

She made him a good wife; and as the years went by she bore him seven children, four boys and three girls, all as beautiful as could be, with white skins and large gentle eyes like their mother, and sturdy limbs like their father.

But though she loved her children, and never complained,

yet the seal-wife cast many a longing glance towards the sea; and often in the twilight she would be down walking along the sands, looking out over the waves, and singing such strange, sad, beautiful songs as brought tears to the eyes of the few who chanced to hear them.

Now it happened that one early evening the farmer went off in his boat fishing; and he took the three elder boys with him, whilst three of the other children went down to the ebb to gather cockles and limpets. But the youngest little girl stayed at home, because, running barefoot, as the children always did, she had cut her foot on some broken glass. So there she sat in a chair by the hearth, with her sore foot resting on a stool.

And what was the seal-wife doing? She was in and out, in and out, searching, searching, looking into cupboards, reaching up to feel along the shelves, stooping to peer under beds, and rummaging among the farmer's clothes.

'Mam,' said the little lass, 'what are you seeking?'

'Oh, my bairn,' answered the seal-wife, 'don't tell any, but I'm looking for a bonny seal-skin to make a soft shoe for your sore foot.'

'Well, then,' says the little lass, 'maybe I ken where 'tis. For one evening, when you were down singing on the sands, and I was in my bed, and my dad thought I was sleeping – but I wasn't sleeping, I was waking – I saw my dad go to stand tiptoe under the slope of the roof beams, and he put up his hand and felt along a beam, and took down oh, such a bonny skin from behind it! He was looking at the skin and stroking it a while with his hand, and then he lays his cheek against it and sighs, and after that he stands tiptoe again and puts it back where it came from, and. . . . Oh, Mam, where are you going in such a hurry? Come back here, and I'll tell you some more!'

But the seal-wife had rushed out of the kitchen and into the children's bedroom: she was up on a chair and feeling with one hand along under the roof beams, feeling, feeling, till her fingers touched something soft. . . . Yes, she had it, her seal-skin! Pulling it down, clasping it close, she ran back into the kitchen.

'Farewell, farewell, my bonny bairn!' she said to the little girl. 'For now your Mam must leave you.'

Hugging the skin to her breast, she rushed down to the sea, flung on the skin and, with a wild cry of joy, plunged into the water and swam away.

Then far out, up from a gentle wave, a seal man rose to greet her; and together they went away and away, now diving down under the water, now lifting their heads above the waves to glance about them, their great eyes shining with the joy that was in their hearts.

And so it was that the farmer, returning from the fishing in his boat with his three sons, saw the two seals. And thus it was that he heard one of them singing:

> 'Good man of the land, farewell to thee,
> I liked thee well, thou wast kind to me,
> But I love better my man of the sea.'

Far away, and farther away, over the water, under the water, swam the two seals. And that was the last the farmer ever saw of his seal-wife. Though often and often, when his day's work was done, he would wander along the sands, watching the sea. But never again did he catch a glimpse of her. No, never again.

8 The little wee man

As I was walking mine alone,
Between a water and a wall,
There I spied a little wee man,
And wow, but that wee man was small!

His legs were but a finger long,
And thick and nimble was his knee;
Between his brows there was a span,
And between his shoulders there was three.

THE LITTLE WEE MAN

He lifted a stone six feet in height,
He lifted it up to his right knee,
And fifty yards and more I'm sure,
I wot he made that stone to flee.

'O little wee man, but you have power,
And O, where may your dwelling be?'
'I dwell beneath yon bonny bower,
O will you go with me and see?'

So on we leaped, and away we rode,
Till we came to a little hall,
The roof was of the beaten gold,
And the floor was of the crystal all.

There were pipers piping in every nook,
And neat wee ladies dancing bonny;
And aye they danced and aye they sang,
'He's been long away, has our wee mannie.'

Out went the lights, down came the mist,
Ladies nor mannie more could I see;
I turned about, and gave a look,
Just at the foot of Benachie.

9 The Black Bull of Norroway

Once upon a time there was a queen who had three bonny daughters, but neither palace nor kingdom, because the king, her husband, had been defeated and killed in battle by a neighbouring king. So now the queen and the three bonny princesses must live in a cottage, and do all their own work like any poor peasants.

Well, one day the eldest princess said to the queen, 'Oh mother dear, what is to become of us all? Will you give me your blessing now, and I'll away to the Wise Woman in the Dell, to ask what fate has in store for me.'

And the queen said, 'Go, little daughter. Go with my blessing.'

So the eldest princess kilts up her skirts and away with her to the Wise Woman in the Dell.

The Wise Woman was sitting before the door of her house, reading in a big book.

The princess curtsied, the Wise Woman gave a nod.

'Good day to you, Wise Woman.'

'Good day t'ye, young princess. And what might ye be wanting of me?'

'Just to know my fortune, if you please, Wise Woman.'

And the Wise Woman said, 'Go in at my front door, and through the house, and out at my back door. Look up the road. Then ye'll see your fortune coming.'

So the eldest princess did that. She went in through the Wise Woman's front door, and down the passage, and out of the back door, and looked up the road. What did she see? She saw a golden coach, drawn by six white horses, coming along the road.

And she ran back to the Wise Woman and told her what she had seen.

'Aweel,' says the Wise Woman, 'ye've seen your fortune. Yon coach and six is coming for ye.'

The princess had only just time to run back home and tell her mother when the coach and six drew up at her mother's door. And out of the coach stepped a handsome prince.

'Welcome to me, my bonny bride,' says the handsome prince.

And he takes the eldest princess by the hand, helps her into the coach, and drives off with her.

Then the second princess said to the queen, her mother, 'Dear mother, give me your blessing, and let me also go down to the Wise Woman in the Dell to ask my fortune.'

And the queen said, 'Go, little daughter. Go with my blessing.'

So the second princess kilts up her skirts, and away with her down to the Dell.

The Wise Woman was sitting before the door of her house, carding wool.

The princess makes a curtsey; the Wise Woman gives a nod.

'Good day to you, Wise Woman.'

'Good day t'ye, young princess. And what might ye be wanting of an old woman?'

'Just to know my fortune, if you please, ma'am.'

And the Wise Woman answered, 'Go in at my front door, and through the house, and out at my back door. Look up the road. Then ye'll see your fortune coming.'

The second princess did that. And when she looked up the road – what did she see? She saw a fine silver coach drawn by six piebald horses coming along the road.

Back she goes and tells the Wise Woman what she has seen.

'Aweel,' says the Wise Woman, 'ye've seen your fortune. Yon coach and six is coming for ye.'

Back home runs the second princess to tell her mother. And there's the silver coach drawn up at her mother's door. Out of the coach steps a handsome prince.

'Welcome to me, my bonny bride,' says the handsome prince.

And he hands the second princess into the coach, and drives off with her.

So now in the cottage there's left only the queen and the youngest princess. And if ever there was a little beauty in this world, the youngest princess is that beauty.

Well, one day passes, and another day passes, and the youngest princess sighs and says, 'Dear mother, I too would know my fortune.'

'Then go down to the Wise Woman in the Dell, and ask of her, little daughter. Go, with my blessing.'

So the youngest princess kilts up her skirts, and away with her down to the dell.

The Wise Woman was sitting before the door of her house, stirring something that bubbled in a great pot.

A nod from the Wise Woman, a curtsey from the princess.

'Good day to you, Wise Woman.'

'Good day t'ye, my bonny lass! And what might ye be wanting of an old woman?'

'Just to know my fortune, ma'am, if so hap you can tell me?'

'Oh aye?' says the Wise Woman. 'Happen your fortune may be coming along the road. Go in at my front door and out at my back door. Look up the road and happen ye'll see it.'

So the youngest princess did that. She went in at the front door, and along the passage, and out at the back door. What did she see? She saw a great Black Bull come rushing along the road, tossing his horned head, and bellowing.

Was the little princess frightened? She was that! All in the twinkling of an eye, she's in again at the back door, and out again at the front, and telling the Wise Woman what she's seen.

'Aweel,' says the Wise Woman, 'ye've seen your fortune. Yon Black Bull is coming for ye.'

Oh no, no! The little princess ran home . . . and there was the Black Bull with his head over the garden gate, and bellowing. The princess had only just time to give one little scream before the Black Bull had her between his horns and was tossing her on to his back, and away with her, and away with her, pounding off along the road the way he had come.

Many's the time she slipped and scrambled off his back, and just as many the times he had her between his horns and was tossing her on to his back again, and she shedding bitter tears all the while, till she was too tired to do aught but sit still, shaking with sobs. And on they went, and on, and she grew faint with hunger.

Then the Black Bull said, 'Feel in my right ear and eat. Feel in my left ear and drink.'

So she put her hand into his right ear and took out a bannock, and she put her hand into his left ear and took out a flask of wine; and for all her terror and her misery, she ate and drank, and felt the better for it. And then it seems she fell asleep, for the next thing she knew, it was night, the stars were shining, and the Black Bull was standing at the door of a great palace.

'This is the palace of my eldest brother,' says the Black Bull. 'And here we shall spend the night.'

Then the palace door opened, and out came two lackeys. The lackeys lifted the little princess off the Bull's back, and brought her into the palace. They set food and wine before her, and she ate and drank. Then came softly-stepping maidens who brought her into a beautiful bedroom, and bathed her tear-stained face with sweet-smelling water, and undressed her, and wrapped her in a soft silken sleeping robe, and tucked her up in bed. And she was so weary that she was falling asleep even whilst they did so; and sleep she did, both long and soundly.

So, in the morning, there were the maidens again, to bathe and dress her, and bring her down to a room where her breakfast was waiting. And oh, and oh, who should be sitting at the breakfast table but the little princess's eldest sister! Now there was laughing and crying, and hugging and kissing! The eldest princess said that the prince her husband, he who had fetched her away in the golden coach, was elder brother to the Black Bull, who, poor thing, was a prince himself – the Prince of Norroway – but enchanted by a demon whom he had once affronted. 'And maybe,' said she, 'it is for you to disenchant him; but of that I know nothing. Only,' says she, 'I have a present for you.' And she gave the little princess a golden apple. 'Keep it carefully,' says she, 'and when you are in the greatest stress that ever mortal was in, then break it, and it will bring you out of it, so I'm told. But just *how* it will bring you out of it, I do not know. . . . And now it is time to say goodbye, for the Black Bull is standing at the door.'

So, when the two princesses had kissed each other many, many times, the lackeys came and brought the little princess out to where the Black Bull was waiting. The lackeys lifted the little princess on to the Black Bull's back, and away and away he galloped with her clinging to his hairy shoulders.

All that day he was running, running; and that day, too, the princess got a bannock out of his right ear, and a flask of wine out of his left ear, and fell asleep, and woke to find the stars shining, and the Black Bull standing at the door of another fine palace.

'This is the palace of my middle brother,' said the great Black Bull. 'And here we must spend the night.'

So all happened on that night as it had happened on the night before. Lackeys came and lifted the little princess from the Bull's back, and brought her into the palace and set food and drink before her. And gentle-handed maidens came and helped her to bed, bathed and dressed her again in the morning, and brought her down to a room where breakfast was waiting. And oh, and oh, who should be sitting at the breakfast table but the little princess's second sister, who said that the prince who had fetched her away in the silver coach was the Black Bull's middle brother. And then again there was laughing and crying and hugging and kissing, and the time seemed all too short before the lackeys came in to say that the Black Bull was waiting at the door.

Then the little princess's second sister gave the little princess a golden pear. 'Keep it carefully,' she said, 'and when you find yourself in the greatest stress that ever mortal was in, then break it, and it will bring you out of it. And now goodbye, little sister, and may all go well with you!'

So the little princess went out to where the Black Bull was

waiting, the lackeys lifted her on to his back, and he set off galloping again, galloping, galloping all through the day, till the sun went down, and the stars shone out, and they came to the door of a third fine palace.

'This palace belongs to me,' said the great Black Bull, 'and it is here that we shall spend the night.'

So again lackeys came to lift her off the Bull's back, and bring her in and set supper before her. And again gentle-handed maidens undressed her and put her to bed, and bathed and dressed her when she woke in the morning, and brought her down to a room where breakfast was waiting. And though the little princess had to breakfast alone that morning, yet she ate and drank with a good heart, for it seemed to her that all must now go well.

Then came the lackeys to tell her that the Black Bull was waiting at the door, and she got up and ran out into the bright sunshine. One of the lackeys gave her a golden plum, telling her to keep it carefully, and to break it only when she was in her greatest need, when surely it would bring her out of it. And so up on to the Black Bull's back again, and galloping away and away, and getting a bannock and a flask of wine out of his two ears when she hungered and thirsted, and falling asleep, and waking again when the sun was setting and the shadows were lengthening, to find that the Black Bull had stopped running, and was standing at the entrance to a deep, dark glen.

'Little princess,' said he, 'light down now, for here I am to go and do battle with my demon. Sit yourself on yonder stone, and keep you still as still; for should you move hand or foot I shall never see you again – and I should be loth to lose you, my little one. Keep a careful watch. If by and by everything about you turns blue, you will know that I have beaten the demon. If everything turns red, he will have beaten me – and then comes the end.'

So the little princess got down off the Bull's back, and sat on the stone. And the great Black Bull walked on down the glen till the sight of him was lost amongst its windings. 'Oh me, what will happen next?' thought the little princess. And she prayed that the Black Bull might win his battle, for indeed she had come almost to love him. And moreover, should he *not* win his battle, but be killed by the demon – what would become of her, alone in this wild place?

So there she sat, still as any statue, for well nigh an hour, whilst the shadows darkened round her, and she heard no sound but the mutter of the wind in the trees. So lonesome it was, so frightening, that she longed to leap up and run, run – anywhere out of this threatening glen!

And then, just when she felt she could bear it no longer, the shadows lightened, and the wind ceased to mutter, and everything about her shone blue as a midsummer sky.

'Oh!' and 'Oh!' And 'Oh, oh, oh! The dear Black Bull has won his battle!' cried the little princess. And in her joy, forgetting that she must not move, she clapped her hands and jumped off the stone.

Alack! Alack! Yes, the Black Bull had won his battle. He was loosed from the spell that the demon had put upon him, he was now a gallant prince, and there he was, hastening up the glen to claim the little princess as his bride. But alack, and alack again, though he sought her high and low, he could not find her: she was invisible to him, and he was invisible to her. And the blue light faded from the glen, and it was now deep night. And still he sought and could not find, and still she waited by the stone, and at last fell a-sobbing from fright and loneliness, and so sank sobbing to the ground, and cried herself to sleep.

In the morning, waking hungry and cold and lonely, she rose up and wandered out of the glen, and on, and on, with naught but high hills round her on every side, and a little winding road under her weary feet.

'Oh, Black Bull,' she cried, 'oh, dear Black Bull, oh, Prince of Norroway, if such you be, come back to me, come back to me!'

But all was still about her, and she got no answer but a mocking echo from the high hills.

So she went, went, went, and came at last to a great mountain of glass that rose up in front of her, blocking her way. She tried to climb that mountain, she tried again and again: but every time her feet slipped from under her, and brought her slithering down.

So at last she gave up, and took a little path along the bottom of the mountain, hoping to get round it at last. But there it still was, ever rearing up on the one side of her; and on the other side of her was a deep swamp where she dare not tread. So on and on and on she went, along the narrow path.

That was the way she was going until noonday; and then she came to a glade under the mountain. In the glade was a cottage, and beside the cottage was a smithy, where a fire was blazing and an old man was working at the forge.

So she asked him where she could find a road to get her over the mountain.

And the old man answered, 'There's nae road over the mountain, lassie. And to walk round it would take ye all your lifetime, for the foot of it stretches for thousands of miles. The only folk who can scale the Mountain of Glass are the folk who wear iron shoes.'

'Oh, then I pray and beseech you,' says she, 'fit me out with a pair of iron shoes! I have no money to pay you, but I will give you the bracelet from my arm, or the gold chain from round my neck, or the ring from my little finger – I will give you one or all of these. For I cannot go back on my journey! And if I cannot go forward, what will become of me?'

'Oh!' says the old smith. 'What should I be doing with your knick-knacks? My work must be paid for by service. Seven years must a body serve me for a pair of iron shoes.'

'Then I will serve you for seven years,' said the princess.

And serve him she did. For seven weary years she cooked

his food, and cleaned his house, and washed and mended his clothes. Her tender little hands grew red and rough, and oh, how often her back was aching! But at the end of the seven years she got her iron shoes; and with them on her feet she was up and over the Mountain of Glass as easy as walking on a highway.

And well, what do you think? When she came down on the other side of that mountain, what should she see, shining in the near distance, but a palace. And that palace was the very one where she had slept on the third night of her travels, the palace belonging to the Black Bull of Norroway himself. And the sight of it lifted her heart.

'Oh, dear Black Bull,' sighed she. 'Oh, royal Prince of Norroway, the roads are long and roundabout, but if they bring me to you in the end, then surely they bring me home!'

And she began to hurry along the road to the palace. But then the nearer she drew to it, the more doubtful she felt. Maybe he would not be glad to see her? Maybe he would be angry because she had failed to do his bidding that time when she clapped her hands and jumped off the stone when she should have been sitting still? No, she would not go to the palace – not yet. 'For if he were to send me away,' thought she, 'my heart would break.'

So she stops in her hurried walk and looks about her; and sees, close by, a little house, with an old woman outside the door bending over a wash tub. And she goes to the old woman and says, 'I am a traveller from a far country and I am sore weary. Would you of your kindness let me bide here for the night?'

The old woman looked up. My word, but she was ugly! Her nose was long, and her eyes were small and squinting, and her yellow cheeks had as many wrinkles in them as a ploughed field has furrows.

'Can ye wash clouts?' says she.

'Yes, I can that,' says the princess.

'Then ye may get your night's lodging,' says the old woman, 'if ye can wash the stain out of this rag of a shirt I'm scrubbing at. My daughter has been at it all morning, and I have been at it all afternoon, but the more we wash, the deeper the stain. It's a blood stain, that's what it is, and an unholy stain, I'm thinking. The shirt belongs to the Prince of Norroway; they say he got it blooded in a fight with the devil, and whether 'tis prince's blood or devil's blood, it's all one: the more we scrub the darker it grows. Come on now – up with your sleeves and take a turn!'

So the princess rolled up her sleeves, and took the dripping shirt between her hands: one little scrub, and scarcely a scrub at that – the stain disappeared.

'Oh my!' said the old woman. 'Oh my!'

And she took the princess in, and gave her a supper and a bed in the garret for the night.

Early next morning, before ever the princess was awake, the old woman ironed the shirt, and stumped off with it to the Prince of Norroway's palace. And wasn't she chuckling! Her ugly face was all one grin. And the reason for her grinning and chuckling was this: after the Black Bull of Norroway had overcome the demon of the glade, and had been restored to his rightful shape, it had been told to him by a good fairy that whoever could wash the bloodstain off his shirt was destined to be his wife. 'And a true and faithful wife she will be to you,' the good fairy had said, 'so see you take no other.'

So then the prince had let it be known that he would take for his bride the one who could wash that shirt clean, be she young, be she old, be she beautiful, be she plain; and many and many were they who had tried, but all had failed.

And now at last the shirt was white as driven snow, and the old woman might well chuckle as she carried it up to the palace, for she was going to tell the prince that it was her daughter who had washed out the bloodstain. And tell him so she did, and showed him the shirt.

62

And the prince, seeing his shirt now white as driven snow, said, 'So be it, she and I will wed.' But he sighed: the old woman's daughter was not the bride he had pictured for himself. However, a prince must keep his word, and the wedding was arranged for the very next day.

So back home goes the old woman, chuckling more than ever, and tells her daughter to prepare herself to get wed. 'And maybe,' says she to the little princess, 'I'll be able to get ye a place as scullerymaid at the palace, for as mother-in-law to the prince I shall have a deal of influence up there, ye may be sure!'

Oh me! Oh me! The little princess went out of the cottage and looked towards the prince's palace. But she could scarce see it for the tears that filled her eyes. 'Dear Bull of Norroway, dear prince, if so you be,' she whispered, 'is it now that I must give up all hope of loving you? Is it now that I must let this old woman find me a place as scullerymaid in your kitchen? No, no, no! Take my farewells and blessings, and I will wander on my way again, praying the good God to bring me home, or to the palace of one of my sisters.'

Then there came to her the remembrance of the golden apple which her eldest sister had given her, and of how her sister had said, 'Keep it carefully, and when you find yourself in the greatest stress that ever mortal was in, break it, and it will bring you out of it.'

'And surely,' thought the little princess, 'I shall never be in greater stress than I am now.' And she took the apple out of her pocket where she had kept it all these seven years, and broke it.

Lo and behold! That apple was full of glittering diamonds! So she shook the diamonds out of the apple, wrapped them in her handkerchief, and took them to the old woman.

'See,' said she, 'all these I will give you if you will put off your daughter's wedding for just one day, and let me watch at the bedside of the Prince of Norroway whilst he sleeps this night. For I have a great curiosity to look upon him.'

63

Oh ho! Oh ho! The old woman would do more than that for a handful of diamonds! ''Tis a queer thing to be asking,' said she, 'but I'll manage it for thee. As the bride-to-be's mother, I'd say they'll be doing what I ask them up there!'

Then she hurried off to the palace and told the prince that the bride's dress was not ready, and that the wedding must be put off till the morrow. The prince was glad enough to agree; he had no wish to marry the old woman's daughter. In fact his heart sank at the thought of it. He said, 'So be it,' and the old woman left him.

Next she sought out a young page whose duty it was to carry up a glass of wine to the prince at bedtime. 'There's a crazy girl down at my place who has a mind to watch by the prince's bed this night,' says she to the page. 'And if we don't allow her, she'll be after me with a knife. So you must let her in. But she shan't disturb the dear prince, oh no! Here's a wee sleeping draught to put in his wine. . . . Now you do as I say, and you shall have a silver coin in the morning.'

The young page, though he thought it all very queer, agreed to do as the old woman told him (for truth to tell, he was afraid of her). And the old woman went back to her cottage to gloat over her diamonds and chuckle to herself about the clever way she had arranged things.

That night, after the Prince of Norroway had drunk off his wine, he had scarcely time to tumble into bed before he fell sound asleep. And the page let the little princess into the room.

The princess stood by the bed and looked down at the sleeping prince. 'Oh, prince,' said she, 'oh, dear Black Bull of Norroway, you said you would be loth to lose me, and sorely, sorely have I grieved at losing you! But now I have found you again, so open your eyes and look upon me, Prince of Norroway!'

And she lifted his hand to her lips and kissed it.

But the Prince of Norroway did not wake.

Long time she stood by the bed, trying to waken him, but all in vain. The hours went by, and still the prince neither woke nor stirred. At last, in her bitter grief, she began to sing. And this is the song she sang:

> '*Seven long years I served for thee,*
> *The glassy hill I climbed for thee,*
> *The bloody shirt I washed for thee,*
> *And wilt thou not waken and turn to me?*'

Over and over again she sang this song. But the prince did not wake. And when the sun rose she went away.

When she got back to the old woman's cottage she thought of the golden pear which her second sister had given her. And of how her second sister had said, 'Keep it carefully, and when you find yourself in the greatest stress that ever mortal was in, then break it, and it will bring you out of it.'

'And if I was in great stress yesterday, I am surely in greater stress today,' thought the little princess. And she took the pear out of her pocket, and broke it.

Behold, it was full of pearls.

So she brought the pearls to the old woman and said, 'See, I am richer than you thought. All these pearls I will give you if you will put off the wedding for another day, and get me to watch beside the Prince of Norroway's bed this night.'

'Oh ho!' said the old woman. 'And isn't it rich I'm growing!'

And off with her to the palace again, to tell the prince that her daughter's wedding-dress was not ready, and that the wedding must be put off for yet another day.

'Oh, for as many days as you wish,' said the prince – a remark which angered the old woman so much that she would have slapped him, had she dared. However, she didn't dare, and she flounced off to find the young page.

'That silly girl will be watching by the prince's bed again tonight,' said she. 'So here's another wee sleeping draught to put in his glass of wine; for the dear prince shan't be losing his sleep because of a foolish hussy. Here's the silver coin I promised you for last night's work; and there'll be another for you in the morning if you do my bidding.'

So that night the prince got his sleeping draught again; and the princess tried to wake him, and could not; and sang her sad little song:

'*Seven long years I served for thee,*
The glassy hill I climbed for thee,
The bloody shirt I washed for thee,
And wilt thou not waken and turn to me?'

Over and over again she sang this song, and the hours of night wore on, and the prince did not wake. So when the sun rose the princess went back to the cottage, weeping bitter tears.

Now all she had left of her three golden fruits was the plum – and what was the use of it? 'When you are in your greatest need, break it, and it will bring you out of it.' Yes, so she had been told. But so she had been told also of the golden apple and of the golden pear, and she had broken them, and they had brought her only sorrow. . . . All the same she broke the golden plum, and found it full of glowing rubies. So she took the rubies and showed them to the old woman, saying, 'All these I will give you, if you will put off your daughter's wedding for just one more day, and arrange for me to watch by the prince's bed this night.'

Oh ho! The old woman would do that! And off she scurried to tell the prince that the bride's dress needed another row of trimming, and that the wedding must be put off for one day more.

The prince gave a sigh of relief, and said, 'So be it.' And the old woman sought out the page, paid him his silver coin for last night's work, and gave him another sleeping draught to put in the prince's wine that evening.

Then home with her, laughing aloud, to spend the day gloating over her diamonds and her pearls and her rubies.

Now that day the prince went out hunting, taking some of his household servants with him. And as they rode along the servants were talking among themselves of the strange sweet singing they had heard for the past two nights coming from the prince's bedroom. And amid the clit-clatter of the horses's hoofs the prince heard their talk, but not distinctly. So he turned, laughing, and said, 'What mystery are you discussing there, my men?'

'Mystery indeed, master,' says one old servant. 'And if it is not making too bold, we would fain know the meaning of it.'

'Meaning of what?' says the prince.

'Of the singing we have heard coming from your bedroom these past two nights, master,' says the old servant.

The prince laughed. 'If you have been hearing things that are not, you must have all of you been making too free with the wine barrel,' said he. 'These past two nights I have slept more soundly than a cradled child. And certainly there has been no singing in my room.'

'Aye, but there has been,' said the old servant. 'And if you have not heard it, master – well, maybe there is a reason for that.'

'A reason!' exclaimed the prince. 'What do you mean?'

'A draught in your glass of wine, maybe?' said the old man.

'*A draught in my glass of wine?*'

'Aye, master, that's what I said.'

'But *why* should there be?'

'Ah master, perhaps we can guess, and perhaps we cannot guess.'

'You speak in riddles!' exclaimed the prince.

'Aye, master, perhaps because I dare not speak more plain. But we think there's mischief brewing. And if she who sings should come again this night. . . .'

'She!' exclaimed the prince. '*She?*'

'Aye, master, 'tis a lady's voice. And the sorrow that's in it bids fair to break a body's heart. If she should sing again

67

tonight, we pray you take heed.'

'I must get to the bottom of this mystery!' said the prince.

'Aye, master,' said the old servant, 'it were well so to do.'

Well, that night, when the page brought the prince his glass of wine, the prince did not drink it. He got into bed, shut his eyes, and feigned sleep; but he was wide awake, and listening.

What did he hear? He heard his door softly open, he heard light footsteps moving across the room, he heard a long sad sigh, he heard a sweet voice singing – oh, so sadly:

> '*Seven long years I served for thee,*
> *The glassy hill I climbed for thee,*
> *The bloody shirt I washed for thee,*
> *And wilt thou not waken and turn to me?*'

'Yes, yes, I will waken and turn to you!' cried the prince. And he started up, and took the little princess in his arms. So between laughing and crying she told him all that had happened to her, and how it was she, and none other, who had washed the bloodstains from his shirt. And he said, 'Now dry your eyes, my darling dear, for tomorrow shall be our wedding day.'

So now all was well. The Prince of Norroway and the little princess were married. The old woman and her ugly daughter were banished. The young page got a good tanning. The little princess's two sisters and their husbands came to the wedding, as also did their mother, the widowed queen. And when the wedding was over, the widowed queen did not go back to her lonely cottage; her home henceforth was in the Prince of Norroway's palace.

10 *Whirra whirra bump!*

A farmer was riding home from market along a lonely road in the twilight when – *whirra, whirra, bump!* – something leaped from the ground on to the horse's back behind him. 'Ha! ha! ha!' With a loud squealing of laughter, that Something was leaping off the horse again, and then on again, on and off, on and off, scaring the horse into a furious gallop.

69

'Hey, hey, whoever you are, this won't do!' cried the farmer. And he flung out a hand, and caught the Something round its fat body.

There it was, held firmly under the farmer's arm, and kicking and squealing for all the rest of the journey. What was it he had caught? It was a young Monster, that's what it was, with the face and form of a five-year-old child, but almost as big as a grown man.

What to do with it? The farmer couldn't decide. But meantime, when he got home, he tied it up with a stout rope to a post in the loft; and there it was, howling like a whole pack of wolves, whilst the farmer went down into the kitchen to get his supper.

But he had scarcely sat down to eat, when there came a heavy *tramp, tramp* out in the yard, and a roaring voice:

> *'My hair is wet, my heart is wild,*
> *Put outside my bonny child,*
> *Or your house, stone by stone,*
> *To all the four winds shall be thrown.'*

'Oh, very well,' shouted the farmer. 'It's glad I am to be rid of him!'

And he went up to the loft, untied the child monster, and dropped him out through the window, shouting 'Catch!' to the huge twilit shape that stood below.

'My Mammy, my Mammy!' cried the child Monster.

'My bairn, my bonny, bonny bairn!' roared the mother Monster. 'But I hope ye've not been chattering? I hope ye've not told the farmer aboot the treasure that lies buried under his hearthstane?'

'I didna tell him anything,' said the child Monster. 'I didna do anything but squeal and greet, and squeal and greet again.'

'So much the better,' said the mother Monster. And off she went, *tramp, tramp*, with the child Monster in her arms, along the road: *tramp, tramp*; *tramp, tramp.*

70

And when the sound of the mother Monster's tramping feet had died away in the distance, the farmer fetched a pick-axe and dug up the stone from in front of his hearth. What was under the stone? A great iron chest. And what did the farmer see inside the chest when he heaved up the lid of it? Gold coins and silver coins, a pile of coins that you might be counting for a week without coming to the end of your counting. So the farmer, who had been but a poor man, was now a rich man, and blessed the day when the child Monster came *whirra, whirra, bump,* jumping on and off the horse's back behind him.

11 Mester Stoorworm

Long, long ago, and longer ago than that, there lived a farmer and his wife who had seven sons. Six of these sons were big strong lads who worked on the farm; but the seventh was a slender, dreamy boy who was nicknamed Assipattle, because he liked to lie among the ashes before the fire and think fine thoughts about the heroes of old and of the valiant deeds they did, fighting monsters and demons, rescuing princesses, and inheriting kingdoms.

Well, that was all very fine for Assipattle, for in his dreams he was the greatest hero of them all; but his brothers bore him a grudge for his idle ways, and as often as they could they dragged him out of his dreams and set him to work on the meanest tasks, hewing wood and drawing water, mixing swill for the pigs, feeding the geese, and such like. And even his mother, though she loved him, was often inclined to fetch him a clout on the ear. But, bless me! – it made little difference to Assipattle, who lived in a world of his own.

So, from year's end to year's end, things went on in the farmer's household, with today much like yesterday, and tomorrow promising little change.

But one day something happened that set the whole country in an uproar, and that was the coming of the huge sea serpent, Mester Stoorworm. Mester Stoorworm's mouth was a mile wide, and as to his scaly body it reached from horizon to horizon. With one snap of his sharp-pointed teeth he could bite a ship into two pieces; and when he was angry his spiked tail lashed the sea into such enormous waves as broke up every ship that sailed, and flung the wreckage far over the land.

Worse than all, the only way to keep Mester Stoorworm in a good temper was to feed him with human flesh.

Oh me – what to do? The king of the country summoned his council. The councillors sat pondering for three days: they suggested this, they suggested that, but they came to no solution. And there was Mester Stoorworm drawing nearer and nearer, vomiting fire, smacking his horny lips, growing hungrier and hungrier, threatening to swallow down every living thing in all the realm.

And on the third day, who should come into the council chamber but the queen. The queen, who was the king's second wife, was no favourite. She dabbled in magic, and had for a friend an evil sorcerer whom everyone feared. But the worst thing about her was her hatred of the young princess, the king's daughter by his first wife, a maiden lovely as a spring morning, and as good as she was beautiful.

Now the queen looked scornfully at the assembled councillors. 'So!' said she. 'For three days you sit here shaking in your shoes! And all your wit is baffled. Send for the Sorcerer: he is the only one who can help us in this extremity.'

The councillors didn't like the Sorcerer any more than they liked the queen, but they sent for him all the same, for they were at their wits' end. So the Sorcerer came, a hideous little man, a regular hobgoblin. And when the Sorcerer told the councillors what they must do, they liked him less than ever; for he said that the only way to save the country was to feed the Stoorworm once a week with seven beautiful young maidens.

'Oh, no, no, no!' cried the king.

And 'Oh, no, no, no!' cried all the councillors.

The Sorcerer shrugged his shoulders. 'Very well,' said he, 'if you prefer the whole country to be laid waste, if you prefer that *all* of you be swallowed down, why then, of course. . . .'

'Surely, surely,' interrupted the queen, 'it is better for a few maidens to die.' But in her wicked heart she was thinking. 'The turn of the princess will come. Oh ho! The turn of the princess will surely come!' (For that is what she and the Sorcerer had plotted.)

And the councillors, with heavy hearts, agreed that if it must be so, it should be so.

What consternation when the news got abroad! Some families with young daughters packed up and left the country. Others locked up their daughters in garrets or cellars, and tried to make out that they didn't exist. All to no purpose: a list of all the young girls between the ages of fifteen and twenty was drawn up; the name of each girl, including that of the princess, was written on a separate piece of paper, the papers were put in a barrel, and the Sorcerer, with his eyes tightly bandaged, put his skinny little hand into the barrel and drew out seven names. But trust the Sorcerer to see through the bandage! And the very first name he drew out was that of the princess.

'Alack! Alack!' and 'Oh, no, no!' Every councillor was up on his feet, crying out that it mustn't be, and it couldn't be. But the king called for silence, and then said, 'Though it break my heart, yet it must be. How can I ask my subjects to sacrifice their daughters, if I am not willing to sacrifice my own? Only let us delay a little, that we may see if there be any champion brave enough to come forward and fight this Monster.'

'That can be arranged,' said the Sorcerer with an oily smile. 'I can cast a spell on the waters that will put the Stoorworm asleep for a little while – for three weeks, per-haps, but not longer.'

The king immediately sent mounted messengers into the neighbouring country and kingdoms, offering the hand of his daughter to any champion who would come forward and fight the Stoorworm. And with the princess would go the kingdom to which she was heir, and also the king's famous sword, Sharp Smiter, which had once belonged to the great god Odin, and against which no mortal man had power.

A beautiful wife, a future kingship, a magic sword – such a tempting offer roused the courage of many a young gallant, and brought thirty-six of them riding post-haste to the palace. But when they looked over the cliff on which the palace stood, and saw, out in the bay, Mester Stoorworm asleep, with his enormous flat head resting on the waves, and his great nostrils breathing out flame and smoke, the young gallants turned round and rode home again.

'For with all the will in the world,' said they, 'it is not possible to fight with such a creature.'

So passed the three weeks, and so came the last evening. And on that evening the Sorcerer said to the king, 'My liege,

75

tomorrow Mester Stoorworm will wake from his sleep. Is
all in readiness?'

'Yes,' answered the unhappy king, 'all is in readiness. The
princess and her six companions are prepared; they are here
together in the palace. The six maidens weep and lament,
but my dear daughter, my brave girl, sheds no tear. Oh
begone, begone – leave me, for I am desperate, and scarce
know what I say, or what I may do!'

The Sorcerer went away. Now it grew late, and in the
palace all was quiet. Those slept who could, and those who
could not sleep lay awake in their beds: all except the king,
who could neither go to his bed nor rest; and with the king
one faithful old retainer, called Donald, who had followed
the king in a thousand battles, and stood waiting to see his
lord to bed.

Up and down, up and down the great hall walked the
king, striking his fists together, uttering prayers, uttering
curses.

'My dear liege lord', said Donald gently, 'it grows very
late. Let me see you to your bed.'

The king didn't answer. He went to a great chest that
stood by his chair of state, lifted the lid, took out Sharp
Smiter, the famous sword of Odin, drew it from its sheath
and laid his hand along the blade. 'Yes, it is still sharp,' he
muttered. 'The years cannot rob it of its power.'

'My dear lord,' said Donald, 'put the sword away. It has
served you well, but your day for fighting is long past.'

The king turned upon his faithful retainer in anger.
'What!' he cried. 'Old I may be – but do you think I will let
my beloved daughter be devoured by a monster and lift no
finger in her defence? I will myself fight this Mester
Stoorworm! He shall swallow down both my sword and me
before he gets my daughter! Be off with you! Go down to
the bay under the cliff, where my little skiff is drawn up
high and dry upon the sand dunes. Run the skiff down to the
water's edge. There anchor her, and see that sail, oars and

rudder are in order. Take a man with you to guard the skiff until the morning, that none may meddle with her. With the first rays of the sun I will set forth to fight. Now get you gone. When you return and tell me all is in readiness, then you shall see me to my bed.'

So, greatly troubled, Donald went down to the little bay, taking with him an old boatman whom he had roused protesting from his bed. Together they ran the king's skiff down into the shallows; and then, having left the old boatman seated in the stern, grumbling about his old bones and the chill of the night, Donald went back to the king to tell him that all was done as he had ordered.

'Thank you, my faithful servant,' said the king. 'And now, for the last time, you shall help me to bed. Oh yes, for the last time, for something tells me that I shall not live beyond tomorrow. What matters? I only pray that when I meet my death, Mester Stoorworm may also meet with his.'

Then Donald, the faithful old servant, wept, kissed his master's hand, and saw him to his bed, as tenderly as he might a little child. . . .

Down at the farm that night the family sat up late, talking excitedly of what was to happen on the morrow. Like all the people in the neighbourhood, they were planning to go early to the cliff-top, that they might watch the sad spectacle of the princess and her six companions cast into the sea to be devoured by Mester Stoorworm. Yes, they were all going except Assipattle, whom they would leave at home to milk the cows and feed the geese.

But when they had at last said all their say and gone to their beds, the farmer's wife exclaimed, 'My, I'm tired! And what with this and that, I'm all of an ache. I doubt if my feet will carry me as far as the cliff-top tomorrow. I think I had best stay home.'

'Stay home!' exclaimed the farmer. 'And miss the sight of a life time! Indeed you shall not stay home! I will saddle my good mare, Swift Go, and take you up behind me.'

But the farmer's wife, who was in a contrary mood, said she didn't want to ride on Swift Go. And when the farmer asked her why not, in the name of heaven, she whimpered, 'Because you make such a mystery of the creature. For five long years I have been begging you to tell me how it is that when *you* ride the mare she goes like the wind, but if anyone else gets up on her back she hobbles along like a broken-down old nag. Yes, for five long years I have been asking you that; and you only answer that you have your own way of managing the creature.'

The farmer laughed. 'Well, well,' said he, 'if it troubles you so much, you shall share my secret. But, mind you, it *is* a secret, and not to be spoken of to anyone else. Give me your promise now that you will not repeat to anyone what I am going to tell you.'

So she promised, and the farmer said, 'When I want Swift Go to stand, I give her one clap on the left shoulder. When I want her to go like any other horse, I give her two claps on the right shoulder. But when I want her to out-gallop the wind, I whistle through the wind-pipe of a goose. And since I never can tell just when I may want her to gallop like that, I always keep the wind-pipe in the right hand pocket of my workaday coat.'

'Thank you for telling me,' said his wife. 'Now I will sleep. And I promise you that no one but myself shall ever know your secret.'

But someone else did know it, and that someone was Assipattle, whose little bedroom was next to that of his parents; and who, since the two rooms were only divided by thin wall boards, could hear every word they were saying.

Assipattle was lying awake, thinking his fine thoughts about the heroes of old, and of the valiant deeds they did. 'If one of those heroes lived today,' thought Assipattle, 'would he not gird on his sword, leap on to his good horse, and ride forth to fight Mester Stoorworm? And is there no such hero alive today? Why, of course there is – *and his name is Assipattle!'* So he got softly from his bed, dressed, softly opened his door, and softly crept downstairs.

In the kitchen he stood and listened. Not a sound now, except for an occasional snore from upstairs in his parents' bedroom. . . . And there behind the door hung the farmer's workaday coat.

Assipattle felt in the right hand pocket of the coat. Yes, there was the goose's wind-pipe, together with the farmer's jack-knife. In one moment the wind-pipe was in Assipattle's pocket, as also was the jack-knife. 'For this hero having no sword,' thought Assipattle, 'a jack-knife will have to serve.'

The next moment he was out of the house and running to the stable; the next moment he was saddling and bridling the mare, Swift Go; the next moment he was leading her out of the stable; the next moment he had his foot in the stirrup. . . .

But the mare was not to be mounted so easily by anyone except her master. She reared, plunged, kicked up her heels: she would have had Assipattle flat on the ground, had he not remembered his father's secret, and clapped her on the left shoulder. Then she stood still as a rock, and Assipattle scrambled on to her back, gave her two claps on the right shoulder, and whispered, 'Off with you, off with you, good mare!' The mare tossed her head, gave a loud whinny, and set off at a round trot.

That loud whinny almost upset all Assipattle's plans. For the farmer heard it, and in an instant was out of bed and flinging on his clothes, and pulling on his boots, and clattering downstairs, and out of the house, and racing down the road, with his six sons racing behind him.

> *'Hi! Hi! Ho!*
> *Swift Go, whoa!'* shouted the farmer.

And when she heard that familiar voice, the mare pulled up with such a jerk that Assipattle all but flew over her head.

But he took the goose's wind-pipe out of his pocket and blew through it with all his might. Save us – what a screech of a whistle! The mare tossed her head, flung up her heels, and off with her, faster than any wind that blows. She was up over the hill and out of sight, with the reins dropped from Assipattle's hands, and he clinging to her mane, before the farmer and his sons had run another three yards. So they had to turn round and go home.

On and on and on, up hill, down dale went Assipattle and the galloping mare, overtaking the wind that blew before them; nor could the wind that blew behind them catch up with them again. Assipattle had recovered his seat, his feet were in the stirrups, his head was high, he was a hero riding forth to do battle, a hero who sang and laughed and shouted in his pride.

In the west the moon was going down; in the east the dawn was reddening. Now here before Assipattle rose the high cliff on which the king's palace stood, and to his right hand lay a little bay, on whose white sands a ripple of small waves broke lazily. Anchored in the shallows lay the king's skiff, with the sail run up and flapping lazily, and an old boatman lounging half asleep in the stern.

All quiet, all peaceful. But look, out there in the deep water slept Mester Stoorworm, his huge head resting on the heave and fall of ocean, his huge body stretching for many a mile under the water, and his great forked tongue lolling out between his half-open jaws. Yes, asleep now, but very soon to wake. . . .

'I must hurry,' thought Assipattle. And he leaped down from the mare's back, hitched the reins round the low branch of a tree, looked about him, and saw, not far from the bay on the edge of a wood, a little one-roomed cottage. Assipattle went to the cottage, found the door unlocked, and pushed it open. A peat fire smouldered on the hearth; in a bed near the fire an old woman lay sleeping, and on a shelf above the fire stood an iron pot.

'By your leave, old lady,' murmured Assipattle. 'And surely you will not grudge an iron pot, nor yet a burning peat from your fire to save the life of the princess!'

And he took down the pot, lifted a burning peat from the fire, put the burning peat into the pot, and tiptoed out of the cottage.

So, carrying the pot, he went down over the sandhills to the sea shore, and hailed the old boatman who sat in the king's skiff.

'Good morrow, friend, good morrow!' he shouted. ''Tis a nippy morning! I think you must be half frozen sitting there. Come ashore now, and take a turn about to unstiffen your legs. I'll mind the skiff for you.'

'Like enough you will!' answered the old boatman. 'And what would my lord the king say, should he come and find me out stamping my feet on the sands, and his skiff left in charge of a scrimmit the like of you?'

'As you will,' said Assipattle. 'I did but speak out of the kindness of my heart. Sit there and freeze if you must, whilst I get busy picking up a few sand-eels to roast for my breakfast. For I've got a rage of hunger on me.'

And he set down his pot, and began scraping about in the wet sand, watched enviously by the old boatman, who felt he could do with some roasted sand-eels himself.

And all at once Assipattle gave a wild leap, clapped his hands together over his head, and shouted, 'Gold, gold, gold! As I live there's gold buried here!'

When he heard that shout, the old boatman scrambled out of the skiff, waded ashore, thrust Assipattle out of the way, and began scraping in the sand with all his might.

Ah ha! What did Assipattle do then? He seized up his pot, jumped into the skiff, pulled up the anchor, grabbed an oar, and pushed out into deep water.

There now was the old boatman, running up and down on the edge of the water, splashing in and out of the shallows, shaking his fists and shouting; and there was the skiff, with the sail billowing in the breeze, dancing over the quiet waves; and there was Assipattle at the rudder, steering straight for the spot where the huge head of Mester Stoorworm lolled above the water; and there now, to add to the boatman's dismay, came the king, riding down over the sand dunes into the bay – the gallant old king, clad in armour, and with the good sword Sharp Smiter at his belt. Behind the king rode his faithful servant, Donald; and behind Donald, at a little distance, in sad procession, came the young princess and the six other maidens, all clothed in white, and riding on small white ponies. And behind the maidens followed a little crowd of the bolder sightseers; though a far bigger crowd was gathering, safe out of harm's way, on the cliff-top, where people from all over the country, some on foot, some on horseback, some in carts and carriages, were now assembling.

There was the old boatman now, fallen on his knees before the king, stammering out wild excuses. But the king was not listening. He had come down to do battle with Mester Stoorworm; now, with the skiff gone, he could only wait and watch. His eyes were on the solitary figure of Assipattle, seated in the skiff, sailing nearer and nearer to the place where Mester Stoorworm lay sleeping. Yes, sleeping now, but soon to wake.

'Ah, the brave lad!' murmured the king. 'The poor brave lad!'

The sun rose behind the cliff, the sun shone in the Monster's eyes, the Monster blinked, opened his eyes, and gave a huge yawn. And when he yawned, a great tide of sea water rushed down into his throat.

And what was Assipattle doing? He was lowering the sail, he was taking the oars, he was rowing the skiff close up to the Monster's head, with the prow pointed straight at the Monster's mouth. Now the Monster's jaws gaped in another huge yawn, another tide of sea water rushed down into its throat; and with the tide went Assipattle, skiff and all.

On and on the skiff was sucked down the great throat with the rush of water, down and down, till the rush of water grew less, and the skiff grounded in the Stoorworm's stomach. Then Assipattle jumped out of the skiff, iron pot in hand, and looked about him.

It was not quite dark, for the flesh of the Monster was covered with a soft weedy sea-substance which shone with a faint silvery light. Assipattle rummaged here, rummaged there, till he came to the Monster's liver.

'It's said that a liver is full of oil,' thought Assipattle. 'So here is where we begin.'

And taking his father's jack-knife out of his pocket, he cut a big hole in the liver, turned his pot upside down, and shook the smouldering peat into the hole. Then he blew with all his might, till the peat began to flame.

The flame, fed by the oil in the Stoorworm's liver, grew bigger and bigger. Assipattle kicked aside the empty pot, and ran for his life to where the skiff lay grounded in the Monster's stomach. Scrambling into the skiff, he waited for what next would happen.

And what did happen was that the Monster, feeling the heat, opened his mouth in a great roar. Then into his mouth and down into his stomach rushed a flood of salt water, and out of his stomach, and up through his throat, and out of his mouth rushed the water again, carrying with it Assipattle, skiff and all, and flinging him, as the flood fell back, high and dry on to the sand of the little bay.

Now earth, sea and sky resounded with roar after roar; and the quiet sea rose into huge wave after huge wave, as Mester Stoorworm writhed and twisted and flung himself hither and thither, and gulped down great draughts of water and spat them out again in his efforts to quench the fires that raged within him. The little crowd of people on the shore fled to join the bigger crowd on the cliff-top, where through the flying foam they watched the terrible turmoil in the sea. Terrible indeed, for the huge body of Mester Stoorworm was cracking and breaking into jagged lumps that were flung hither and thither along the surface of the water; until, when the turmoil at last died down, all that was left of Mester Stoorworm was a scatter of islands, which men now call the Orkneys and the Shetlands, and one larger island which is now called Iceland, and where the fire that Assipattle kindled still burns under the mountains.

Now Assipattle was indeed the hero he had so often pictured in his dreams. The king flung his arms round the lad's neck, and kissed him with tears streaming down his cheeks. He put Odin's sword, Sharp Smiter, into Assipattle's hand, he gave his daughter, the beautiful little princess, to Assipattle to be his wife. He proclaimed Assipattle his heir. Side by side, and followed by a cheering multitude, the king and Assipattle rode back to the palace.

Now when the wicked queen, looking out of a window, saw the joyous procession approaching, she turned on the sorcerer in a rage. 'Is this what comes of all your scheming?' she shrieked. 'Call yourself a sorcerer! You are nothing but a doddering old fool!' And she clenched her fist and struck the Sorcerer in the face. But he snatched her up, wrapped her in his cloak, and flew with her out of the window.

And what became of them after that nobody knew, nor did anybody care.

All was now a joyous bustle, preparing for the wedding of Assipattle and the princess, who were married as soon as might be.

Assipattle rode to church on Swift Go, with the king and the princess driving in a glass coach at his side. But after the wedding Assipattle gave Swift Go back to the farmer.

As to the old woman whose iron pot he had taken, well, he couldn't return that pot to her, for it was buried somewhere among the mountains of Iceland. But she got a new pot instead, and the new pot was filled with gold pieces to the brim; so that the old woman blessed the day when Assipattle had come tiptoeing into her cottage unawares.

12 Flitting

Once upon a time, the very naughtiest Brownie in the world took it into his head to go and live in the house of a farmer. The farmer was well-to-do; he owned flocks and herds and cornlands and grazing lands; everything prospered with him. But there, he could get no peace, because of that Brownie, who racketed about all night long, knocking over

86

tables and chairs, breaking the crockery, upsetting the bowls of milk and cream in the dairy, pelting the walls with the newly made pats of butter, and pinching the maids in their sleep till they woke screaming.

So, since the farmer couldn't get the Brownie to go from the house, he decided to go from it himself, and to move all his goods and chattels to another house that he owned – a house that stood empty at the other end of his farmlands.

No sooner thought of than set about: the farmer and his wife got busy packing, the farm-hands got busy loading up carts and moving all the gear to their new home. By the end of a week the new home was ready, and the old home left empty and desolate; and on a bright spring morning the farmer and his wife, who were the last to leave, got into a cart piled high with luggage – including the churn – and drove away from their old home, which was blazing merrily, because the farmer in his anger had set fire to it.

So away they drove; and at the top of a rise in the road, the farmer pulled up and turned his head to look back at the smoke and flames of his old home, and to shake his fist at the impertinent Brownie, whom he had never set eyes on.

'And may you enjoy yourself making merry among the ruins,' said he. 'You may fling about the ashes to your heart's content, for all I care!'

'Aye, I suppose it's for the best,' said the farmer's wife, wiping away a tear, 'but it sorely grieves me to be seeing what I see. It was a bonny house.'

So as they paused there, gazing at the burning building, she in tears and he in anger, a neighbour who was riding along the road pulled up at the side of the cart.

'So you're flitting?' said the neighbour.

And a little squeaky voice answered from inside the churn, 'Och aye, we're flitting.'

13 The Loch Ness Kelpie

A Kelpie is a monster who lives in a loch; but it doesn't eat fish. No: it eats human beings. And when it comes out of the water it takes the form of a horse, sometimes grey, sometimes black, with a white star on its forehead. Such a beautiful horse, so tame and gentle-seeming, that footsore weary travellers, plodding on their way, are tempted to mount and ride it. Yes, it is quite willing to be ridden, and there it is, all ready, saddled and bridled. So up with you, my lad, or my lord, or my lady, into the saddle! And then what happens? Once you are up, you cannot get down; and off gallops the Kelpie to its loch, plunges with you into the water – and gobbles you up.

Now one of the biggest and fiercest of all the Kelpies was the Kelpie who lived in Loch Ness – the number of unwary folk that this Kelpie had already carried off and devoured was terrifying.

But there was a brave man, called James Macgregor, who was determined to put an end to that Kelpie's mischief. And one day as Macgregor, who had been on business to the town, was trudging home along a lonely road, what should he see but a black horse with a white star on its forehead grazing on the grass by the roadside. The horse was saddled and bridled, and as Macgregor passed by it gave a gentle whinny.

'Oh ho!' says Macgregor to himself. 'Oh ho, my beauty, now is the time to go warily. I ken some things are not what they seem to be!' And he passed by the horse without turning his head, went to lean against a rock a few paces farther along the road, and there drew his sword from the scabbard, and waited.

Now what is the black horse up to? Grazing peacefully, yes: but ever moving closer and closer to the rock where Macgregor is waiting. Oh ho! Oh ho, my beauty! . . . Now the black horse is quite close to the rock; and in a flash Macgregor seizes the horse's bridle with his left hand, swings the sword with his right hand, cuts the bridle strap in two, and pulls that bridle off the horse's head.

What happens? It is now no horse that stands facing Macgregor. It is a monster Kelpie in human shape, black as coal, and with glaring fiery eyes.

'Give me back that bridle!' roars the Kelpie.

'Not I!' says Macgregor.

'Give it back, give it back!' roars the Kelpie again.

'Not I,' says Macgregor again. 'Stand away from me, or my good sword will be cutting through other things, besides the bridle strap.'

Then the Kelpie began to whine and whimper. 'It's *my* bridle! I have done you no harm. Why should you keep what is mine, not yours?'

'It seems I have taken a fancy to this bridle,' said Macgregor.

'But, my friend,' said the Kelpie, 'the bridle is dangerous. It will bring evil upon you. Hold it up now, and peek through the ring of the bit. Then you'll see the evil that threatens you.'

So Macgregor held up the bridle and looked through the ring of the bit. What did he see? The air around him was thronged with demons.

'Be off!' shouted Macgregor, with a swing of his sword. And immediately the demons vanished.

Macgregor laughed. 'It seems your threatened evil is but faint of heart,' said he to the Kelpie.

And he walked on his way, with the bridle in his one hand, and the drawn sword in his other hand, and occasionally turning to brandish the sword at the Kelpie, who was following him step by step, muttering threats and curses.

So on they went, and on they went, and at last came in sight of Macgregor's house. And then the Kelpie screamed out, 'James Macgregor, I am setting it on you as crosses and spells that you and the bridle shall never enter your house together.'

'And I am setting it on *you* as counter spells,' said Macgregor, 'that you come no nearer to me, now or hereafter now, than the length of my arm and my drawn sword.'

'Warlock!' screamed the Kelpie.

'Botcher!' laughed Macgregor.

Then the Kelpie gave a leap right over Macgregor's head, and came down an arm's length and a sword's length in front of him; but between him and the house.

Macgregor laughed again. 'My friend,' said he, 'is it thinking to enter my house that you are? Yes, my wife is in there alone, and maybe you are smacking your lips at the thought of eating her for your supper? But you cannot enter my house, for a bunch of rowan hangs over the front door, and another bunch of rowan hangs over the back door; and rowan, as you know, protects the house from all such unwelcome visitors as demons, warlocks, ghosts, witches, and kelpies.'

'Then do let us be reasonable,' said the Kelpie. 'Granted I cannot enter your house. But by the crosses and spells I have put upon you, neither can you enter the house with my bridle in your hand. Therefore return my bridle to me. Then you can go into your house, and I will depart and trouble you no more.'

'When I reach the house it will be time enough to think about that,' said Macgregor. And he walked on leisurely, with the Kelpie darting from one side of the road to the other, and now in front of Macgregor, now behind him, but ever keeping an arm's length and a sword's length away from him, and screaming out, 'You shall never enter your house with my bridle! My bridle and you shall never enter your house together!'

'You need not deafen me with your skirling,' said Macgregor calmly. And so came to his house and stood for a moment thinking what next to do.

Then he looked through the open parlour window and laughed. For inside, under the window, sat Mrs Macgregor, darning a pair of her husband's socks.

'A good wife is a protection against all the Kelpies in the world,' said Macgregor. 'Catch!' he cried, and flung the bridle through the window into her lap.

Mrs Macgregor looked up startled. And well she might be startled, for the Kelpie gave a yell that shook the house.

'You've beaten me this time, you warlock!' yelled the

Kelpie, and fled away into the night.

Macgregor then opened his front door and went into the house. He hung the bridle over the parlour fireplace; and when he wanted to know what was happening in the invisible world of demons and suchlike, he had only to take the bridle down and look through the ring of the bit to have that invisible world revealed to him. By this means he was able to save himself and many other folk from a host of troubles. He became known as Macgregor the Wizard, and did much good.

And what became of the Kelpie? Well, he plunged back under the waters of Loch Ness. And there he remains to this day, feeding no more upon human flesh, but upon fishes. For without his bridle he can never again lure unwary travellers to their doom.

14 Short Hoggers

For many and many a year – for more years than anyone
living could remember – the good people of Whittinghame
had been troubled by a ghost. Night after night this ghost
would be running to and fro, to and fro, from a large elder
tree at one end of the village to the graveyard at the other
end of the village; and all the time it would be crying out:

'*Wae, wae is me, wi-oot a name,*
I canna get going frae Whittinghame!'

What sort of a ghost was it? Well, not a very frightening one, you would think: just the ghost of an innocent little child, whose cruel stepmother had murdered it, and buried it under the elder tree. And that had happened generations ago. The cruel stepmother was dead and gone to her doom this many a year; but still the little ghost ran through the village street at night, crying out its 'Wae me'. It scared the good people of Whittinghame, that it did, and no one had the courage or the kindness to stop it in its running and ask what ailed it, or how it could be given help, or how it had come about that such an innocent-seeming little spirit hadn't, in the usual manner, gone up to heaven straight away to take its rest in Paradise.

Well, of course the little spirit *had* gone up to heaven, and knocked at the Gate of Paradise. And Saint Peter himself had opened the gate, and looked out. Saint Peter was holding a big book in one hand, and a quill pen in the other hand, and the first thing he said was, '*Name please?*'

'I have nae name,' answered the little spirit.

'But,' says Saint Peter, 'no one can come in here without a name, because every soul has to be entered in my book. You must go back down to earth, my dear, and get you a name, before I can let you in.'

So then Saint Peter clangs the gate shut, and the little spirit sinks down to earth again.

And there it was, as I have told you, night after night, week after week, month after month, year after year, running through Whittinghame from the elder tree to the graveyard, and from the graveyard back to the elder tree, to and fro, to and fro, and crying out its 'Wae's me'.

And through the years it grew thinner and thinner, and wispier and wispier, and paler and paler; and though it had once worn a pretty little coat and neat shoes and stockings, its little coat was now in rags, its little shoes had worn out and fallen from its feet; and as to its stockings – there was so little left of them that they looked for all the world like those

94

footless short socks that folk used to wear as gaiters, and which go by the name of *hoggers*.

And no one, no one would help it. Because everyone believed that if you spoke to a ghost you would immediately die and become a ghost yourself. So it seemed as if the village of Whittinghame was doomed to be haunted till the end of time.

But, by good luck, there had recently come to live in Whittinghame a merry fellow called Sandy Macdougal, who was as often drunk as sober. And late one night, Sandy, having spent a happy evening at the inn and filled himself up with a variety of mixed drinks, was reeling home by the light of the moon, and roaring out a song. So, as Sandy was passing the graveyard, who should come running towards him but the sad little ghost.

Sandy was feeling well-disposed to all the world, whether ghost or otherwise; so he stopped in his wavering course, looked the little ghost up and down, stared at its footless ragged stockings, laughed, touched his cap, and called out, 'Evening, evening! And how's all wi' ye, this braw evening, *Short Hoggers?*'

Sandy didn't wait for an answer. He went on his way chuckling. Nor did he heed the exultant cry of the little ghost:

> '*Oh weel's me the noo, I've gotten a name,*
> *They ca' me Short Hoggers o' Whittinghame!*'

And up rose that little ghost, up and up, up over the village, up into the moonlit sky, up and up to the Gate of Paradise, to knock at the gate, and have it opened by Saint Peter, book in hand.

'Well, my dear,' says Saint Peter, 'and have you a name?'

'Short Hoggers, Short Hoggers o' Whittinghame,' cried the little spirit; '*that's* my name!'

So Saint Peter wrote the name in his book, opened the gate wide, and let in the little spirit to take its joy and peace in Paradise.

15 Seven Inches

There was a king in Scotland who had three daughters, very lovely; but the youngest was the loveliest of the three. And there came to woo them three princes, very handsome; but the youngest prince, who wooed the youngest princess, was the handsomest of the three.

So on a sunshiny morning, the king, the three princesses,

and the three princes went to take a walk together by the lochside. And out from behind a clump of grasses jumped a tiny mannie, no more than seven inches high. The tiny mannie was making a doleful face, and holding out his tiny hand a-begging.

'Be off with you, little rascal!' said the king.

And, 'Be off with you, little rascal!' said the two elder princes.

And, 'Be off with you, little rascal!' said the two elder princesses.

But the youngest princess said, 'Ah, don't be speaking so rough to the poor wee Seven Inches.' And she broke off a pearl from her girdle, and put it in the wee mannie's hand. And though it was but a little pearl, it was a big gift to Seven Inches.

'And here's something else for you,' said the youngest prince. And he took a small gold coin from his pouch, and put it in the wee mannie's other hand.

'Ho, ho! Ha, ha!' That wee mannie, Seven Inches, scampered off with never a backward look.

Then the king, and the three princesses, and the three princes strolled on along the margin of the loch. And when they had turned a corner round a belt of trees, what should they see, drawn up against the bank, but the beautifullest boat in all the world, white as ivory (and maybe 'twas ivory itself) with masts of gold and sails of silver, and a green flag with a white lily on it drooping from the masthead.

'Oh,' says the eldest princess, 'I'll take a sail in that fine boat!'

And, 'Oh,' says the second princess, 'I too will take a sail in that fine boat!'

But the youngest princess said, 'I don't think I'll take a sail in that fine boat, for I doubt it's an enchanted one.'

'Coward!' says the eldest princess, stepping aboard.

And, 'Coward!' says the second princess, stepping aboard after the eldest.

'Come weal, come woe,' says the youngest princess then, 'I'll be called coward by no one!'

And she steps into the boat after her sisters.

The king and the three princes were about to follow them when – see now! – up out of nowhere on to the deck jumps the wee mannie, Seven Inches, bidding the king and the princes stand back.

'*What!*' says the king. '*You* give orders to *me!*'

And he thought to draw his sword, but his arm went numb – he could no more draw his sword than he could fly. And when the three princes tried to draw *their* swords, their arms went numb too.

And it wasn't only their arms that went numb: it was their legs also, so that they couldn't stir from where they stood. There they must stand, and there they must stare, and hear Seven Inches give a shrill call, '*Ho and away!*' and watch the silver sails fill, and the boat glide off over the clear waters of the loch, with the reflections of the boat, all white and gold and silver, going along through the water beneath it.

The three princesses stretched out their arms and cried, 'Help, oh help!' But Seven Inches said, 'Wisht, wisht with your screeching! To those who deserve good fortune, good fortune will come; but to call for help will wreck the boat.'

So then the three princesses were quiet; only they shed a few tears.

The loch was not very big: the king and the three princes, though they couldn't stir from where they stood, could see plainly to the other side of the water. They saw the boat ground, and Seven Inches and the three princesses step out of it: and then they saw Seven Inches letting the princesses down by a white basket into a hole in the earth, and jumping down into the hole after them. And when there was no more sight of either the princesses or Seven Inches, the strength came back into the arms and legs of the king and the princes, and they ran, ran, round the loch and came to the hole in the earth.

By the hole was a windlass with a silk rope wound round it, and the white basket fastened to the rope; and each of the princes thought of nothing else but to jump into the basket and be let down into the hole to rescue the princesses. But the basket would only hold one of them: and since they were quarrelling about who should go down, the king said, 'Eldest first.'

So the eldest prince got into the basket, and the others let him down, telling him that when he was ready to come up again, he should give a tug at the rope. They took turns at the windlass, unwinding the rope, and they unwound yards and yards of it, till they had unwound it all. And then they stood and waited.

They waited for one hour, they waited for two hours, they waited for three, four, five hours: but there came no pull on the rope; so they wound up the basket again, and it was empty. They went away then, greatly troubled. And the king set guards by the windlass to watch all night.

Next day the second prince was let down in the basket; but he didn't come up again either, and the king was half out of his mind with grief and distraction. So, on the third morning, the youngest prince went down. And, if it please you, we will go down with him, and see what happened.

Down he went and down into a deep and silent darkness – he might have been sewn up in a black bag for all he could see or hear. But at last there came a glim of light and then a radiance, and a prattle of running water. The basket bumped to a stop, and the prince stepped out of it.

Where was he? In the Other World. In a green meadow, scattered over with flowers. A stream flowed sparkling through the meadow; there was a singing of birds among trees; the sun shone brightly, and in the distance the white walls of a palace stood up boldly against a blue and cloudless sky.

So off hurried the prince over the meadow grass, and came to the palace: and since both courtyard gates and hall doors were open, into that palace he went, passing from one grand room to another grand room, till he came to a dining-hall where a fire blazed on the hearth, and food and drink were laid out on a long table.

The prince had a wish to sit down and eat, for he had a great hunger on him; but, 'No,' he thought, 'I must wait till I'm invited, for that is only mannerly.' So he sat down by the fire and waited.

Well, he hadn't waited long before he heard the sound of footsteps, and with the footsteps a *pit pit pattering* of some-thing as small and light as the hop of a bird. Then the door, which he had left ajar, was pushed wide open – and who should come in but the youngest princess, with Seven Inches holding to the hem of her robe, and pattering in along with her.

Oh, to be sure, there they were now, the prince and the princess, laughing for joy and hugging and kissing; and not taking much notice of Seven Inches who watched them thoughtfully.

So by and by Seven Inches takes a jump, lands on the table, and looks round at the dishes. 'I don't see anything eaten here,' says he to the prince. 'Is it dwining and dwindling you are, that your appetite's gone from you?'

'No, indeed,' says the prince. 'I'm hungry enough. But I thought 'twas only manners to wait till I was invited.'

'Ho!' says Seven Inches. 'Those two other princes didn't think so. They snatched at the food, they did, without a by your leave or if you please. Gave me rude answers too, when I asked them whose table they thought it was. Ha! ha! I doubt if they'll be feeling hungry again for a while. See those two curtains in the corner yonder? You take a look behind them.'

The prince stepped over to the corner and drew back the curtains. Oh horror – what did he see? The two princes turned into marble statues!

'Well, never fash yourself about *them*,' said Seven Inches.

'Sit you at the table now, and we three will take our dinners.'

So the prince and princess sat down and ate. And Seven Inches hopped about the table, and helped himself to a morsel here, and a morsel there. It was a delicious meal, though neither prince nor princess could enjoy it as much as they should, being troubled about those two statues.

But they were together, and that was all that really mattered to them. So when they had eaten, Seven Inches sent them out into a pretty garden, and there they wandered hand in hand until the evening, when Seven Inches called them in to supper, and after that showed them to their beds.

Next morning there was a good breakfast waiting for them, with Seven Inches hopping about on the table among the dishes. And after breakfast Seven Inches said to the prince, 'Today you'll be setting out up the valley. You'll be going for some time, and then you'll come to a giant's castle. You'll find the eldest princess in that castle, and you'd better bring her away with you. But first you'll go on to another giant's castle, where you'll find the middle princess, and you can bring her along also. And should the giants chase after you, as most like they will, I'm giving you these two little knives. Throw one behind you at the first chase, and throw the other behind you at the second chase, and you won't have any more trouble with either giant. Now be off with you: don't stand there making eyes at your sweetheart; the sooner gone, the sooner back. Meantime your sweetheart is safe enough with me.'

So away went the prince, walking, walking all day up the valley; and weary and footsore and hungry he was when he came in sight of a great stone castle, with the sun going down red behind it. And he went into the castle and found the eldest princess there. She was sitting on a stool, shedding tears, but she cheered up when she saw him, and gave him a good supper.

Well, he'd scarcely finished eating when there came *tramp*, *tramp* outside, and the castle walls shuddered. 'Oh me,' says the princess, 'it's the giant!' And she pushed the prince into a cupboard, turned the key on him, and put the key in her pocket. Then in stamped the giant, huge and horrible.

He was sniffing and snuffing. 'I smell raw meat!' he bawled. 'Bring it out! Bring it out!'

'It's your supper meat you're smelling,' says she. 'And if it was raw this morning, it's cooked now, so sit you down and eat it.'

'It smells raw!' said he.

'It's only a bit underdone, and that's the way you like it,' says she. 'But it seems there's no pleasing you.'

So he grumbled a bit, and then he gobbled up his supper, rubbed his great hand across his ugly mouth, and said, 'When will you marry me?'

'On St Tibb's Eve,' says she.

'I wish I knew when that was,' said he, yawning.

'You'll know soon enough,' said she. 'Go to bed.'

'No,' says he, 'I'll not!'

And there he was yawning and blinking and muttering about St Tibb's Eve, till he fell asleep with his head in the dish.

Soon as the giant was asleep, the princess let the prince out of the cupboard.

'You best be going on right away to the other giant's castle, where my middle sister is,' said she. 'And when you come back I'll be waiting for you with a good horse under me.'

So, tired as he was, the prince set out once more, walking through the night, and coming to the other giant's castle in the grey of dawn. This giant was still in bed and asleep, but the second princess was up, kindling the fire and getting the giant's breakfast ready. And oh, the joy that brightened on her face when the prince walked in!

She took him to the stables, where they saddled and bridled two fine horses; and it was up on the horses' backs and away that they were in a twinkling. But going through the castle gates one of the horse's hoofs struck against a stone, and the clitter-clatter that it made woke the giant, who was a light sleeper, and he jumped out of bed with a roar and gave chase.

The horses galloped, the giant ran, but the great strides that the giant took were outpacing the horses; and he was reaching out his long arm to catch one of them by the tail, when the prince remembered the knives Seven Inches had given him. So he flung one of those knives behind him. Then out of the knife sprang up such a dense and thorny thicket as took the giant some time to push his way through; and by the time he had got clear of the thicket, the prince and the second princess had come up close to the castle of the other giant. And there under a hedge, they found the eldest princess mounted on a fine horse, and waiting for them.

So, without stop or stay, away with the three of them, galloping, galloping. But the giant who had got clear of the dense and prickly thicket was coming along behind them, and roaring like thunder. His roars brought the other giant out of his castle, and now there were the two giants pounding with great strides after the riders, and catching up on them every moment. So the prince threw the second knife behind him, and where the knife fell, the earth gaped, and there was a great deep gully, a mile wide, with the bottom of it filled with black water.

The giants leaped into the water, but it was so deep that it was going over their heads; so they scrambled out and ran round on the bank. But by the time the giants were round the gully, the prince and the two princesses had reached the palace of Seven Inches; and all about that palace Seven Inches had laid a charm which no one could pass unless he wished it. So let the giants roar and bluster as they might, they could do nothing but turn round and go home.

Well, well, there was gladness for the two elder princesses in being free, but there was sadness and a shedding of tears again, when they saw the marble statues of their two lovers. But by and by in comes Seven Inches and taps those statues with a little rod, and turns them back into flesh and blood.

'And may it be a lesson to you to behave more courteously in future,' says Seven Inches. 'Though I don't suppose it will,' says he, 'for I haven't much hope of you.'

However, for the time, everything was well. And they all sat down together at the long table and had a good breakfast.

After breakfast Seven Inches took them all into his treasure chamber; and the gold and the silver and the precious stones that were piled up in that chamber you'd never believe, short of seeing them. It was 'Oh!' and 'Ah!' and blinking their eyes that they were, with all the splendour and the glitter of it.

'Well, leave gaping,' says Seven Inches; 'this is what I brought you in to see.' And he pointed to three gold crowns that stood by themselves on a small round table. Inside each gold crown was a silver crown, and inside the silver crown was a copper one. 'These are for you,' says he to the three princesses, and he gave one set of crowns to each of them. 'Keep the crowns safe, my dears,' says he, 'for you are to wear them at your weddings, and those weddings must be all on the same day. Should you be married on different days, or should you be married without your crowns, a mischief will fall on you, and an uncanny mischief it will be – so take heed to what I say. . . . And now it's time, and more than time, that you were away home. You'll find the basket at the bottom of the pit to carry you up into the world. Give a tug or two at the rope and you'll be hauled up; for the king has set sentinels to watch by the windlass night and day.'

Well, they all said goodbye to Seven Inches and set off for the bottom of the pit, each princess going arm in arm with her prince.

The youngest prince and princess were going last; and they hadn't gone far before the youngest princess said, 'Oh, there's a stone got in my shoe!'

So she stopped to take off her shoe, and the youngest prince stood by her. And then, waiting till the others were well ahead, the princess handed him her crowns to hold and whispered, 'Dear love, I'm thinking your brothers mean no good to you. I'm thinking they plan to do you a mischief. I'm thinking they will make for you to come up last in the basket, and I'm thinking you had best not get into it, but put in a big stone instead. Then we shall see what will happen. No, I won't take back my crowns. Keep them safe under your cloak; for did not Seven Inches say I was to be married in them? And by my troth I will wed none but you.'

So then they walked on, and overtook the others, and all came to the bottom of the pit where they found the white basket lying.

Well, the eldest princess stepped into the basket, gave a twitch on the rope, and was hauled up, and greeted by a great cheering and shouts of joy from the sentinels who worked the windlass. The shouts and the cheering were echoing down the walls of the pit, and putting heart into those who were waiting their turn to go up. So to the sound of that cheering the basket came down again, and the second princess was hauled up in it, and then the third. And after her the eldest prince went up, and after the eldest the second. And now there was the youngest prince standing alone at the bottom of the pit, and thinking of what his princess had said.

So, when the basket came down yet once again, the prince didn't get into it. He took up the biggest stone he could find, put the stone in the basket, and pulled on the rope. Up went the basket: but it hadn't gone up half way when down it came again in a rush. With the force of its falling both basket and stone were broken to pieces; and if the prince hadn't leaped out of the way, he would have been broken in pieces also.

Now what to do? Nothing but to go back to Seven Inches's palace. So that's what he did, and looked for Seven Inches to ask for advice. But though the prince searched high and low, both inside and outside the palace, not a sign of Seven Inches could he see. And in that palace he lived lonely for a week, and more than a week, finding food and drink and all things he needed; but never finding Seven Inches however much he searched and called.

Then one morning he went into the treasure chamber. And on the small round table, where the crowns had been, he saw a beautiful gold snuff box lying. He picked up the snuff box and opened it, and well, what do you think? Out of that snuff box bounced Seven Inches, and hopped on to the table.

Seven Inches was laughing. 'I think, prince,' says he, 'it's wearying of my palace that you are?'

'Not of the palace,' says the prince. 'If I had but my princess with me, I would ask nothing better than that we should stay here with you for the rest of our lives.'

'Well, you're wanted up above,' says Seven Inches. And he hops back into the snuff box. 'You're to shut down the lid on me,' says he, 'and put me in your pocket. When you want my help, you've only to open the lid. Got the crowns safe? Well, keep them so. And now clap the lid on me, and take a walk down the garden. What I like about you is that you do as you're told.'

The prince did do as he was told, though he couldn't see what good would come of it. He shut the snuff box, put it in his pocket, and so, with the three crowns under his cloak, he went out into the garden. He was going down a gravel path with a thorn hedge on either side, and feeling none too happy, when the path gave a turn – and where was he?

Where indeed! Up in the world again, and on a road he knew well; for but a mile or two away was the king's palace; and at the roadside was a blacksmith's forge that he had often strolled past on his way to the lochside with the princess. But, goodness me, he was all in rags: and though he had the three crowns under his cloak, that cloak was as dirty and tattered as any beggarman's.

So as he stood there, all in amaze, the blacksmith came out of his forge and looked him up and down. 'Ech, sirs!' says the blacksmith, 'a lusty lad like you tramping the roads, when there's so much work needs doing! Come, give me a hand at the forge. There'll be meat and drink for you, and a few pence at the end of the week, if you do your work well. Are you willing, or are you not willing?'

'I'm willing,' said the prince. And he went into the forge, and set to work with the bellows for the smith, who was making horseshoes.

So, when they had been working for some two hours, the smith said, 'Enough for now,' and they both went outside and sat on a bench. The smith fetched bread and cheese and beer from his kitchen, and gave the prince a good share. And there came a tailor along the road and sat down beside them.

'Strange happenings in the kirk,' says the tailor. 'It's wedding day up there, as you know, and I was up with all the world beside, to look on.'

'And a braw sight, surely!' said the blacksmith.

'Aye and no,' says the tailor. 'The two princesses were a braw sight, with their triple crowns on their heads, and their jewel-decked robes. And the two bridegrooms were a fine sight, walking up to the altar in their doublets and hose all a-glitter with gold and gems. But the youngest princess was a sad sight, standing by a pillar in a coarse grey hodden gown, with the new-shed tears still glistering on her bonny cheeks.'

'Aye, poor lassie,' said the blacksmith, 'she might well shed tears, seeing how her prince met his death, so they say, when the rope broke and let the basket fall with him in it. But these strange happenings in the kirk – what were they?'

'Well,' says the tailor, 'there were the two princes, all so grand, as I said, marching up to the altar as if they owned the world. And they hadn't got but a few more proud steps to take when – *whirra, whirra, bang!* – the ground under their feet opened, and down they went, *ker-flump*, into the vaults where the coffins are kept.

'A pretty hurly-burly there was in the kirk after that, with the screeching of the ladies, and the running and pushing of the wedding guests to peer down the hole, and the shouts of *"Help, help"* coming up from them below, and the priest, white as a ghost, and muttering out a prayer or two, and carpenters bringing in ladders with a "Make way there, make way!" and nobody making way: though they got the two princes up at last – all covered with cobwebs and mould they were, and well bruised, no doubt. But the long and the short of it is that the weddings are put off. For it seems there's a doom that the three princesses must all be wedded at the one time, and all wearing their three crowns.'

'And the youngest princess is keeping her three crowns safe, no doubt,' said the blacksmith.

'Ah, no,' said the tailor, 'the poor lassie hasn't got them. She'd handed them to her sweetheart, seemingly; so they went down with him in the basket. And it's all witchery, for the hole in the earth has closed up, as if it had never been, and the windlass gone too. Now the king has given out that whoso can make three crowns, the image of the others, shall wed the poor young princess. So here's a chance for you, Master Blacksmith.'

'For me?' laughs the blacksmith. 'If it were three horse-shoes I could manage it – but three crowns the like of those! Nay, nay, I doubt there's a smith in the world has skill enough for that.'

Then the prince, who had all this time been listening and saying nothing, spoke up. 'I should like to have a try at making those crowns.'

'*You!*' says the blacksmith.

'Yes, I,' says the prince. 'I'm handy at such things. If you'll get me one crown for a pattern, and a quarter pound of gold, a quarter pound of silver, and a quarter pound of copper, and leave me to myself in the forge this night, I doubt not but that by sunrise I'll have the three crowns ready for the youngest princess – bless her dear heart!'

'Well, I wish that you may!' says the blacksmith. And he hurried off to the palace, got the gold and the silver and the copper from the king, and also the pattern crown. And with these things the prince locked himself up in the forge that evening. He was hammering, hammering, hammering from then till sunrise, and a crowd of folk gathered outside the forge to listen. They were getting on each other's backs to glimpse through the windows; but all they could see was the glare from the forge, and the dark figure of the prince, stooping over the anvil with his hammer.

Every now and then he would come to the window and throw out a fragment of gold or silver or copper, which the folk outside scrambled to pick up. 'He's breaking everything to flinders, the young gowk,' they said. 'He'll never fashion those crowns!'

But in the dawning out he comes, with the pattern crown in his one hand, and the three crowns, gold, silver and copper, one inside the other, in his other hand. (For he had kept them all the time, you see, safe wrapped in his cloak, as the princess had bidden him.)

Then from the crowd such a roaring cheer went up as you might have heard from John o'Groats to Stranraer; and when he could make himself heard the prince asked the blacksmith to carry the crowns up to the palace, being too shy to go himself, seemingly. So away went the smith, with all the crowd at his heels, and gave the crowns to the king.

'So now you shall marry my youngest daughter,' says the king – greatly relieved in one way; but in another way, maybe, not much wanting a blacksmith for a son-in-law.

'Hech, sirs!' says the blacksmith. 'I'm a married man already. And come to that, 'twasn't I made the crowns; 'twas a young fellow that but yestermorn came to work for me.'

'Oh,' says the king, 'I hope he's respectable!' And he sent

for the youngest princess, and asked her was she willing to wed the man who had made the crowns.

'Let me see those crowns,' says the princess.

So she took a good look at them, and laughed, and clapped her hands. 'Yes, yes,' says she, 'I'll marry the man these crowns came from. I'll marry him soon as may be. Only send for him, dear Father, send for him!'

So the king called the eldest prince and told him to go in a carriage to fetch the crown-maker to the palace. But when the eldest prince heard that it was to a blacksmith's shop he must go, he said he must have two carriages, for he wasn't willing to ride in the same carriage as a blacksmith's apprentice.

So he got his two carriages, and came to the blacksmith's: and there was the 'apprentice' standing at the forge door. He was looking grimy and tousled after his night in the forge. The eldest prince gave him but one quick glance, and quickly looked away again. For grimy and tousled as he might be the 'apprentice' reminded him of his youngest brother. And to be reminded of a body you think to have murdered is not pleasant.

'Are you the fellow who made the three crowns?' says the eldest prince disdainfully, with his chin in the air and his eyes on the clouds.

'Yes, I am that fellow.'

'Then perhaps you'll give yourself a brush and step into the hindmost carriage,' says the eldest prince, 'for the king wishes to see you.'

Well, the youngest prince stepped into the hindmost carriage, never bothering to brush himself first, and away went both carriages on the road back to the king's palace. And they hadn't gone far before the youngest prince took the snuff box from his pocket and opened it. Then out hopped Seven Inches and stood on the prince's hand.

'What's your will?' says Seven Inches.

'Little lord,' says the prince, 'I would wish to be back in

the forge. And I would wish this carriage to be filled with paving stones.'

'Right!' says Seven Inches.

And in a moment there was the prince sitting in the forge, and the horses tugging at a carriage suddenly gone heavier than heavy.

Those horses were sweating when they got to the palace, where the king himself was standing on the steps, waiting to greet his new son-in-law. He came hurrying down the steps too, and himself opened the carriage door. And no sooner was the door open than *clatter, clatter, clatter* – a shower of stones came pouring out, knocking the king down.

Well, he wasn't hurt except for a cut here and there, and a bruise or two – but wasn't he angry! 'What's the meaning of this?' says he to the eldest prince, wiping the dirt from his face.

'I have no idea,' says the eldest prince haughtily. 'The fellow got into the carriage, and we haven't stopped on the way. I regret what has happened, but it is not my fault.'

'It *is* your fault, it must be your fault!' said the king. 'You must have been rude to the man and angered him. A fine one you to send on messages!' And he called the second prince and said, 'Go you to fetch the blacksmith's apprentice, and see that you're civil.'

So the second prince set off, and he behaved just as haughtily as the eldest one; for he too thought it beneath his dignity to be civil to a blacksmith's apprentice. He rode in one carriage, and had the 'blacksmith's apprentice' riding in another carriage behind him. And when they arrived at the palace, and the king hurried to open the door of this second carriage, it was a shower of mud that poured down over him, which made his majesty very angry.

'You're no better than your brother!' said he to the second prince. 'A fine couple of sons-in-law I'm going to get with the pair of you! It's in my mind to send you both home, only my girls will not forgive me if I do. Now it seems I must go and fetch this apprentice myself, but I'll not take two carriages: the blacksmith's apprentice shall sit by my side, since, come weal, come woe, he's to be my son-in-law.'

So, after the king had washed the mud off himself, and changed his clothes, he set off in a fine carriage for the forge.

The prince, the 'blacksmith's apprentice', all grimy and tousled, was standing at the door, and when he saw the king coming the prince quickly opened the snuff box, and Seven Inches hopped out on to his hand.

'What now?' says Seven Inches.

'Little lord,' says the prince, 'I would that on the drive to the palace the king might fall asleep. And I would that when he wakes he might find me brushed and combed, and dressed as befits my rank.'

'That shall be done,' says Seven Inches.

Well, the carriage drew up at the forge door, and the king looked out. Then says he, 'Are you the lad who made the three crowns?'

'I am the lad who sent them,' says the prince. 'And if I didn't make them, I don't know who did.'

'Enough of that!' says the king. 'Step into the carriage now, and sit beside me. My youngest girl is waiting for her bridegroom.'

So the prince stepped into the carriage, and they set off back to the palace. The king was nodding and yawning, and by and by he fell asleep. He didn't wake up until they reached the palace; and when he did wake up – what did he see? No dirty apprentice, but the prince whom everyone had mourned for dead: a prince brushed and combed, fresh as a spring morning, and dressed as fine as could be.

The first thing the prince did, after he had paid his respects to the astonished king, was to run and find his princess. And joyous they were, the pair of them, as you may well believe.

But the other two princes weren't joyous, because of their

guilty consciences. However, the three weddings were held as soon as might be, with each princess wearing her three crowns. And after the weddings the two elder princes went off with their brides to their own kingdoms; and the youngest princess and the youngest prince stayed with the old king.

But when the prince opened the snuff box to thank Seven Inches for all he had done, he found the snuff box empty. Seven Inches had gone back to his palace in the Other World. Nor was he ever seen on earth again.

16 In a sack

Sandy McTavish took a sack and went to town to sell some fish he had caught. And after he had sold his fish he bought this and that in the market, and then stepped into a baker's shop for a loaf of bread. On the counter of the shop was a trayful of newly baked curranty cakes, and the smell of those cakes made Sandy's mouth water. Some of those curranty cakes Sandy must have! Well then, he still had money in his pocket, so why didn't he buy a few? Just because Sandy wanted something for nothing – he was like that.

So, the baker happening to step into the back for a moment, what did Sandy do? He snatched up two good handfuls of those cakes, stuffed them into his sack, and off with him on the road to home.

He had a long way to go, for his home lay on the other side of a mountain; so there he was, toiling up the mountain, with his sack full of provisions, including the curranty cakes, slung across his back. The sack was heavy: every now and then Sandy would sit down beside the path for a bit of a rest, and then on with him once more. And he had just taken one such rest, and was toiling on his way again, when he heard a squeaky voice calling out of the bracken at his feet, 'Gibbie, Gibbie, what are you doing? Gibbie, Gibbie, where are you going?'

And, bless me, if out of the sack another squeaky voice didn't answer:

> '*In a sack*
> *On a back,*
> *Riding up the mountain!*'

Was Sandy scared? He was! He snatched the sack off his back, flung it down, and ran, ran, pelting up that mountain as fast as his legs would carry him.

Then out of the sack hopped a little Brownie man; and up from under the bracken jumped another little Brownie man. And the two of them sat down cross-legged and gobbled up all Sandy's stolen cakes.

17 The seal-hunter and the mermen

There was once a man who earned his living by hunting seals and selling their skins. He wasn't a poor man, because he was the best seal-hunter on the coast, and he was able to keep his wife and children in comfort.

In the sea on that coast there were a great many seals, and they used to come out of the water and bask on the rocks under the seal-hunter's cottage. So it was easy enough for him to kill them, poor things. And he didn't trouble his head with feeling pity for them. He had always killed seals, you see; it was his living, and that was that.

Amongst the seals there were some which were much larger than others. And the country people said to the seal-hunter, 'You shouldn't kill those big seals! Don't you know they're not really seals at all, but mermen and merwomen? They have a country of their own under the sea; only they take the form of seals when they come up to lie on the rocks.'

But the seal-hunter said, 'What nonsense are you talking? They are seals right enough; and they are the most worth killing of all their kind, because their skins are so large and soft and fine that I can get a much better price for them than for ordinary seal-skins.'

Now one hot day, when the seal-hunter stepped out of his cottage to go about his work as usual, he saw among the seals on the rocks a really huge fellow, the biggest seal he had ever seen in his life.

'Ah ha!' thought he. 'That animal's skin will be worth something!'

So, with his big sharp hunting-knife in his hand, he went down to the rocks, slipping cautiously from behind one rock to behind another rock, taking care to make no noise and to keep himself hidden, till he came to the flat ledge where the seals were basking. Then he made a leap, and before the seals had time to dive into the water, he lunged with his knife at that biggest seal of all. But his foot slithered on some wet seaweed, he stumbled, the knife left his hand, and with a great cry of pain the big seal dived into the water and disappeared, with the knife sticking in his side up to the hilt.

The seal-hunter was furious with himself, both because of his clumsiness and because of losing his precious knife. He went home to dinner in a very bad temper; and since his temper was no better after his dinner, he took a walk out along a moorland road to cool his head.

He hadn't gone far when he saw a very tall man riding towards him on a gigantic grey horse; and he jumped into the side of the road to let the stranger go by, wondering in his mind who he could be.

'No countryman of ours,' he thought. 'A foreigner surely! But then, what country in the world can breed such enormous horses? . . . And the rider is richly dressed, too; he looks like a prince. But what can a foreign prince be doing here in our wild stretch of country, where we are far from any town, and where no one lives except farmers and fishermen?'

So, standing back at the side of the road, the seal-hunter took off his cap and made a low bow to the strange gentleman.

But to his astonishment, the stranger pulled up.

'Good day to you, seal-hunter,' he said. 'For I think that is your trade?'

'Good day, my lord,' said the seal-hunter. 'Yes, that is my trade.'

'I am travelling in search of seal-skins,' said the stranger. 'I can give you an order, now, for a hundred skins of the best quality.'

What an order! The seal-hunter was delighted. 'Give me a few days,' he said, 'and I will supply you.'

'A few days!' exclaimed the stranger. 'I must have the skins tonight!'

'*Tonight*, my lord! But that is impossible! The seals won't come out of the water again until tomorrow morning.'

'Tush!' said the stranger. 'I know where there are any number of seals. Get up behind me, and I will take you where they are.'

So the seal-hunter got up behind the stranger. The stranger shook his bridle rein, and away galloped the great grey horse at such a pace that the seal-hunter could scarcely keep his seat.

They galloped, galloped, and so fast they went that the

119

world streamed away under the horse's hoofs. Where they went, whether north, south, east or west, the seal-hunter couldn't have said. The speed made him feel giddy, and the country they passed through seemed to him quite unfamiliar. And then, all at once, the stranger pulled up with such a jerk that the seal-hunter slid off the great horse and landed on his hands and knees.

'Here we are!' said the stranger.

Merciful powers! They were on the edge of a huge precipice that went down and down and sheer down, hundreds of feet into the sea. The seal-hunter crawled to the edge of the precipice and peered over. If there were seals lying on the rocks down below – how could any man get at them?

But there were no seals, there were no rocks; there was only the blue sea breaking in foam against the cliff.

'Where are the seals you told me of?' he asked fearfully.

'You will see presently,' said the stranger, who had dismounted and was standing at the seal-hunter's side.

The seal-hunter was feeling frightened. Why had he been brought to this wild and lonely spot? Who was this tall stranger? Was he man – or was he fiend? The seal-hunter turned to run from the place; but the stranger caught him up in his arms, and flung him over the precipice – down, down and sheer down into the sea.

Splash!

'Now my last hour is come!' thought the seal-hunter, as his head sank under the waves.

But to his astonishment he found he could breathe quite easily under the water. The stranger had leaped in after him and was close at his side, and they were going down and down and ever down as rapidly as they had galloped on land. But there was something different about the stranger; he was the same, and yet not the same: his face was the same, his arms were the same, but his legs – he had no legs, his body ended in a fish's tail!

'What are you?' gasped the seal-hunter.

120

'I am as you see me,' said the merman, for such indeed he was. 'Come, don't be distressed! You have a tail yourself.'

And to his horror the seal-hunter found that this was true. He had been turned into a merman.

'Oh, what shall I do?' he thought, almost in tears. 'This artful creature has laid a spell upon me! Now I shall never see my home again, or my wife, or my little children! I have done nothing to deserve this – but I am doomed, doomed!'

Down they went, and ever down, till they came to a great arched door of pink coral, which opened and let them through. Now they were in an immense hall, whose walls were gleaming mother-of-pearl, and whose floor was silver sand.

'Here are your seals,' said the merman.

The hall was full of them: huge creatures like the one the seal-hunter had wounded on the rock ledge. But even as he looked at them, they changed their shape; now they were seals, now they were mermen and mermaids, and again they were seals. None of them made a sound; they looked terribly sad, and the hall was absolutely silent; but they swam up and peered into the seal-hunter's face, and swam away again, shaking their heads sorrowfully.

'Wait here,' said his guide, the one who had brought him. And he moved away, and disappeared through a door at the end of the hall.

When he came back he had a knife in his hand.

'Have you seen this before?' he said, holding out the knife.

Yes, the seal-hunter *had* seen that knife before! It was his own hunting-knife. Now he thought he understood it all. They had brought him down here to have their revenge on him, to kill him with his own knife! His mouth went dry and his whole body trembled.

'I . . . I was but following my trade!' he stammered.

But instead of killing him, they crowded about him. The seals rubbed their soft noses against his face, the mermaids and mermen stroked and caressed him. And now at last they spoke. No harm should come to him, they said. They would love him all their lives, if he would but do what they asked him.

'Tell me what it is!' said the seal-hunter. 'I will do anything – anything you wish me to do, if it is in my power!'

'Then follow me,' said his guide, and led him through the door at the end of the hall, and into a small room, where, on a bed of green seaweed, lay a great brown seal with a gaping wound in his side.

'That is our king,' said his guide, 'whom you tried to kill this morning, though you had been warned by your friends that you should not do so. You had been warned that the great seals are not mere animals, but mermen and mer-women with speech and understanding such as you human beings have. I have brought you here to anoint his wound, for no hand but yours can heal him.'

'I will willingly anoint his wound,' said the seal-hunter. 'But I have no skill in healing. And oh, forgive me, for I did not know what I was doing!'

'The healing of our king will bring forgiveness,' answered the merman. 'Here in this pitcher is pure water; here in this casket is salve for anointing. Do what you can.'

The seal-hunter went over to the bed, and washed and anointed the terrible wound. And, incredible as it seemed to him, at the touch of his hands the wound gradually dis-appeared. Very soon there was only a small scar left; very soon there was not even a scar, and the big seal sprang up, as well as could be. Nor was he any longer a seal; he was a majestic merman king, with an emerald-green body and a golden tail, and a diamond crown on his head.

The king went into the great hall, and his subjects crowded about him, rejoicing, cheering, laughing, clapping their hands. But the seal-hunter crept into a corner. His mind was a blank of misery. True, they had forgiven him, they were not going to kill him, but – to remain down here in this

strange guise for the rest of his life; never to breathe the
good air, never to see his home again, never again to look
into the eyes of his wife, or fondle his children – how could
he bear it?

But presently, to his great joy, the king called him and
said, 'You are now free to go home to your wife and children.
Your guide shall take you; but only on one condition.'

'Oh, what is the condition?' cried the seal-hunter. 'I will
agree to anything – anything!'

'That you will take a solemn oath never to kill or wound a
seal again.'

'I take my solemn oath,' said the seal-hunter. 'I give you
my promise; and I will keep my promise.'

A great sigh of relief went up from all the company when
he said those words.

'Then farewell,' said the king. 'And if you keep faith with
us, we will keep faith with you.'

The seal-hunter didn't know what the king meant by this.
But he knew that it was no small thing that he himself had
promised. For with that promise he had given up his liveli-
hood. But he thought that once he was back on earth in his
proper shape, he could turn his hand to some work that
would at least keep him and his family from starving.

And so, with his guide going before him, he passed from
the hall and through the arched door of pink coral, and up
and up through the shadowy water that gradually grew
lighter and lighter, until there they were again in the sunlit
waves under the great cliff.

With one spring they reached the top of the cliff, where
the big grey horse was waiting for them, quietly nibbling the
turf. Their merman shapes had fallen from them, and they
were now as they had been before, a plain seal-hunter and a
tall lordly stranger.

'Get up behind me,' said the stranger, swinging himself
into the saddle. 'And hold tight.'

The seal-hunter scrambled up and took a firm grip of the

stranger's coat; the stranger shook the bridle, the horse galloped off, and the world flew from under his hoofs at such a speed that the seal-hunter turned faint and giddy. But in less than no time it seemed, there was the horse pulling up with a jerk at the seal-hunter's garden gate.

'Goodbye,' said the seal-hunter, sliding down from the horse's back and holding up his hand. 'I think you have let me off more lightly than I deserve. Though indeed I erred in ignorance.'

But as the seal-hunter reached up, the stranger stooped and handed him a heavy sack.

'Fair is fair,' he said. 'No one shall say that we took away an honest man's living, and left him penniless. Here is what will keep you in comfort to your life's end.'

And with those words he vanished, horse and all.

Staggering under its weight, the seal-hunter carried the sack into his cottage. He heaved it on to the kitchen table, untied a seaweed rope from about its neck, and turned it upside down. Oh hark! Oh see! *Clitter-clatter*, and *glitter-glitter!* Out of the sack golden coins, and more golden coins came tumbling. By the time the sack was empty the table was heaped from end to end with bright new sovereigns!

Now the seal-hunter was able to buy and stock a large farm. And that farm he and his family worked with a will; so that they all lived in comfort to the end of their days.

18 The Strange Visitor

A woman was sitting at her reel one night;
And still she sat, and still she reeled, and still she wished for
   company.
In came a pair of broad broad feet, and sat down at the
   fireside;
And still she sat, and still she reeled, and still she wished for

company.

In came a pair of small small legs, and sat down on the broad
broad feet;

And still she sat, and still she reeled, and still she wished for
company.

In came a pair of thick thick knees, and sat down on the
small small legs;

And still she sat, and still she reeled, and still she wished for
company.

In came a pair of thin thin thighs, and sat down on the thick
thick knees;

And still she sat, and still she reeled, and still she wished for
company.

In came a pair of huge huge hips, and sat down on the thin
thin thighs;

And still she sat, and still she reeled, and still she wished for
company.

In came a wee wee waist, and sat down on the huge huge
hips;

And still she sat, and still she reeled, and still she wished for
company.

In came a pair of broad broad shoulders, and sat down on
the wee wee waist;

And still she sat, and still she reeled, and still she wished for
company.

In came a pair of small small arms, and sat down on the
broad broad shoulders;

And still she sat, and still she reeled, and still she wished for
company.

In came a pair of huge huge hands, and sat down on the
small small arms;

And still she sat, and still she reeled, and still she wished for
company.

In came a small small neck, and sat down on the broad broad
shoulders;

And still she sat, and still she reeled, and still she wished for company.

In came a huge huge head, and sat down on the small small
   neck.

'How did you get such broad broad feet?' quoth the woman.

'Much tramping, much tramping' *(gruffly)*.

'How did you get such small small legs?'

'*Aih-h-h!* – late – and *wee-e-e* – moul' *(whiningly)*.

'How did you get such thick thick knees?'

'Much praying, much praying' *(piously)*.

'How did you get such thin thin thighs?'

'*Aih-h-h!* – late – and *wee-e-e* – moul' *(whiningly)*.

'How did you get such big big hips?'

'Much sitting, much sitting' *(gruffly)*.

'How did you get such a wee wee waist?'

'*Aih-h-h!* – late – and *wee-e-e* – moul' *(whiningly)*.

'How did you get such broad broad shoulders?'

'With carrying broom, with carrying broom' *(gruffly)*.

'How did you get such small small arms?'

'*Aih-h-h!* – late – and *wee-e-e* – moul' *(whiningly)*.

'How did you get such huge huge hands?'

'Threshing with an iron flail, threshing with an iron flail'
   (gruffly).

'How did you get such a small small neck?'

'*Aih-h-h!* – late – *wee-e-e* – moul' *(pitifully)*.

'How did you get such a huge huge head?'

'Much knowledge, much knowledge' *(keenly)*.

'What do you come for?'

'FOR YOU!' *(At the top of the voice, with a wave of the arm
   and a stamp of the feet.)*